One Blue Shoe

Molly Garcia

Copyright © 2023 by Molly Garcia

All rights reserved.

No portion of this book may be reproduced in any form without written permission from the publisher or author, except as permitted by U.S. copyright law.

Contents

Dedication		V
1.	Chapter One	1
2.	Chapter Two	11
3.	Chapter Three	20
4.	Chapter Four	30
5.	Chapter Five	46
6.	Chapter Six	54
7.	Chapter Seven	59
8.	Chapter Eight	66
9.	Chapter Nine	76
10.	Chapter Ten	79
11.	Chapter Eleven	86
12.	Chapter Twelve	92
13.	Chapter Thirteen	100
14.	Chapter Fourteen	104
15.	Chapter Fifteen	113

16.	Chapter Sixteen	121
17.	Chapter Seventeen	129
18.	Chapter Eighteen	135
19.	Chapter Nineteen	139
20.	Chapter Twenty	146
21.	Chapter Twenty-One	150
22.	Chapter Twenty-Two	159
23.	Chapter Twenty-Three	164
24.	Chapter Twenty-Four	172
25.	Chapter Twenty-Five	174
Afterword		178
Also By		179

For Hannah
My Daughter & My Muse

1

Chapter One

Chris tried to ignore his wife and focus on the road ahead.

The stifling hot weather had finally broken with a storm. It was dark, and rain lashed the windscreen so hard that the wipers were having trouble clearing it quickly enough for him to see much further ahead than a few inches.

He set his gaze on the running water and blurred glass, peering out at the hazy road ahead.

Julie was spitting words at him like poisoned darts, each one designed to hit its target in the way only someone who'd practiced through years of marriage could achieve.

His wife was well-versed in exactly what to say, and tonight she was throwing everything in her arsenal at him.

"I don't know why you bothered; you clearly didn't want to be there with me. Half the night tapping on your phone, and then complaining about the cost loud enough for the waiter to hear."

Chris wasn't sure why he bothered either, the stupid marriage counselor had suggested it, a date night to get to know each again he'd said. More like the date from hell, if they weren't married, he'd have told her goodnight before the starters had even arrived.

He tuned back into her voice to find that Julie wasn't finished. Oh no, Julie had a good bit of bile to spew yet. They weren't far from home but it was plenty of time to get in the last digs.

"And then just to add one last humiliation, as though the slurping and noisy chewing wasn't enough, you refuse to leave a tip."

Just in case Chris still hadn't got the picture Julie added one last barb.

"Cheap bastard."

He turned slightly in the driver's seat to glance at his wife's face. Despite being contorted with anger, her blue eyes were flashing, and with her cheeks flushed he could still see her beauty and remember why he'd fallen for her.

Back when she'd saved her ire for subjects she was passionate about it had been a turn-on, now she aimed it at him, and he was sick of feeling like he wasn't good enough.

After keeping his mouth closed for as long as possible, he retaliated.

"Just fuck off Julie, I've had a fucking 'nuff of you. I've got half a mind to just dump you out of the car here and you can walk your sorry self home in the rain."

"That'd be just like you, chuck me out in a fucking storm. Perfect fucking end to a shitty night."

Chris was still glaring at her and was just about to make another comeback when he felt something smash into the bonnet. As he slammed his foot down on the brakes the car slid across the road. Chris fought with the steering wheel until they finally came to a jerking halt.

It was too dark to see what he'd hit in his mirrors. Sitting in silence for a moment he steadied his nerves to go and check.

Chris used the torch app on his mobile to see as he got out of the car. The thin hood on his jacket was no protection against the torrent of rain and he was soon soaked through.

The light bobbed along the road and at first all he could see were potholes full of water. But as he lifted his phone slightly, he caught a glimpse of what looked like a heap of something about a yard away.

Chris was almost reluctant to get closer, he wasn't sure he wanted to know what it was or see the damage that his car had done to it.

Forcing himself forwards, it wasn't until he was right on top of the heap that he realised it was actually a person. One wearing a dark blue hooded top, denim jeans, and baby blue sneakers.

He felt the vomit rise in his throat.

"Fuck, shit, bollocks."

Chris hadn't realised that Julie had joined him until she spoke.

"Shit."

She squatted down next to the prone form and placed two trembling fingers on the girl's long pale neck before shaking her head at him.

"She's definitely dead Chris."

He blanched and took a hasty step backwards.

"What am I going to do Julie?"

She shot him a hard stare

"What do mean, what are you going to do? Call the police of course."

Chris hung his head gulping big breaths to try and stop himself from being sick.

"What if they breathalyse me?"

Julie narrowed her eyes and stood back up.

"You only had a couple of glasses of wine at the restaurant."

Chris's drinking was yet another reason for Julie's carping at him, but there was no point in lying, not now.

"I might have had a few beers while you got ready and a shot or two of vodka."

"For fucks sake Chris. Not again."

He'd had a drink-drive conviction a few years ago, they'd taken away his licence for a humiliating two years. Two years where Julie was the only driver and he'd had to rely on her for lifts everywhere.

Julie looked away, and he could almost hear the cogs churning. Julie was always the one to come up with the answer, the way out.

She looked back at him, her face hard and set as she held up her hand and used her fingers to demonstrate.

"We've got three choices as I see it. One, we call 999 and face the consequences when they find out you're over the limit. Two, we call them and tell them I was driving, I had one and a half glasses of wine and would pass the breath test."

Julie stopped and Chris frowned at her.

"What about option three?"

She shrugged, "You won't like it. Three, we do nothing. In fact, if we move her off the road it'll be ages until anyone finds her. It's rural around here and not many people use this route."

Chris's mouth dropped open in shock, but then he heard a calm voice in his head.

If you let her take the blame she'll have a hold over you forever, you'll never be rid of her. If you tell them you did it, you'll lose everything. At least if you take door number three, she'll be as guilty as you. That'll keep her mouth shut."

Julie read his expression, and just as she always did, knew what choice he'd made.

She gave him a sharp nod.

"You take her shoulders and I'll grab her feet. Head into the field and we'll push her under that hedge."

Chris was on autopilot; it was as though he was watching himself doing this grisly task and not really taking part.

He gripped the girl's shoulders, but as he lifted, her head lolled back revealing her long, white neck. Her dark shoulder-length hair ticked the exposed skin on his hands. He noticed she had a small tattoo of a flower on the inside of her wrist before looking away. Chris shuddered, but not wanting Julie to think he was wimping out started taking large steps backwards.

The ground was boggy and sucked at his feet, so he focused on making sure he kept his balance and avoided looking at the young girl's face. He could hear Julie panting and cursing as she tried to lift her feet out of the sodden ground without losing either of her shoes.

When they finally arrived at the hedge, he quickly dropped his end, eager not to be touching her.

Julie tutted but miraculously refrained from saying anything cutting as she usually would. They both stood there for a moment while they caught their breath.

The young girl was crumpled in the wet grass, her hair had fallen over her face and Chris found it easier to look at her now he couldn't see her empty eyes staring at him.

He bent down ready to push her under the hedge, but as he put his hands out, he noticed that Julie had tucked her hand into the girl's pocket and removed her purse. Pulling out an ID card she read it out to him.

"Daisy Landsbury, 22 years old.

Chris stared at his wife in horror.

"Why the fuck do we need to know that?"

Julie shrugged. "Might be useful to know what we're dealing with"

Without another word, they rolled the young girl under the hedge and Chris was grateful to see that she'd landed with her back to them. No need to look at that dead, accusing face, he thought.

They walked back to the car in silence, his hand was trembling so hard he couldn't hold the keys. Without a word, Julie took them, got in the driver's side, and fired up the engine.

He could feel her glances all the way back, but he resolutely stared out of the windscreen and avoided meeting her eye. Hypnotised by the motion of the wipers he tried to push the image of that girl's face out of his head.

Their street was empty, it was after midnight, and with the terrible weather, there wasn't a soul about to see them arrive. He was fairly sure the nosy old woman two doors up twitched her curtains. Logically it didn't matter if she saw them arrive home but the guilt made him twitchy.

Julie unlocked the front door, and he followed her over the threshold where he unlaced and then kicked off his saturated shoes.

His socks clung unpleasantly to his feet and his clothes were stuck to his skin, he shivered and moved closer to the radiator for warmth.

Julie looked him up and down, he glanced down at himself and saw his clothes were not only soaked through but covered in thick mud.

"Get those off and bag them up, we'll burn them when it stops raining. I'll do the same."

Julie padded to the kitchen and came back with two black bin liners and handed him one.

"Put it all in there so it doesn't contaminate the carpet."

Chris turned his back to her; despite a decade of marriage, he was suddenly revolted by the idea of her seeing him without clothes.

He snagged a hoody from the coat peg in front of him and wrapped it around himself before turning around again. Julie had also completed her strip and had a coat protecting her nudity.

She snatched his bag out of his hand and dumped them both by the backdoor before wordlessly running upstairs. A few minutes later he heard the shower running, and Chris slowly plodded up the stairs himself.

In their bedroom he sat on the end of the bed they'd shared for the whole of their marriage, even the recent problems hadn't separated them physically at night. He shuddered, the thought of sharing a bed with her now made his skin crawl.

It was her fault

The voice announced this, and he found himself nodding in agreement.

If she wasn't shouting and causing a fuss you'd have been concentrating, and you wouldn't have hit that girl.

Chris narrowed his eyes at the bathroom where his wife was busy using up all the hot water, he snatched up his dressing gown. He'd use the other bathroom to wash up and then sleep in the spare room tonight.

In fact, he thought, he'd probably move in there permanently.

When Chris opened his eyes, it took him a moment to work out where he was.

The spare room, he realised as he took in the plain magnolia walls and nondescript prints they'd hung to try and add some colour.

He'd thought he'd never get off to sleep last night, but a combination of the alcohol and the adrenaline from the incident must have put him out in the end.

A picture of that girl's face popped, unwanted, into his head and he pushed it away.

That girl has a name

The mocking voice of his conscience, but Chris refused to give it headroom. He was not going to say her name, even to himself.

The atmosphere in the kitchen was decidedly frosty. Julie threw him the bog-eye a few times before slamming a mug of coffee in front of him hard enough to slop the contents over the tabletop.

Apparently, that was his fault too.

Julie threw a cloth in his general direction, never an especially good aim she hit him right in the face. Then again, he thought ruefully, maybe that's exactly what she'd been aiming for.

He dabbed up the brown liquid, and since Julie wasn't speaking to him decided he'd catch up on the news on his phone while he drank his coffee.

Opening the app he scrolled down the various depressing headlines. Road accidents, stabbings, the economy was shot to shit, and yet another MP had made an inappropriate comment on social media.

Chris was about to move on to his reading app when one headline caught his eye, it was under the section reserved for "your local news."

CAN YOU HELP?

22-year-old Daisy Landsbury hasn't been seen since yesterday evening and her family is appealing to anyone who knows her whereabouts to contact them.

"Daisy went out after tea but never returned home, this is so out of character for her. If anyone has seen her, please let us know she's safe. Daisy, if you're reading this, we just want to know you're okay."

The police don't believe there are any links between Daisy's disappearance and that of fourteen-year-old Tilly Thorpe.

Chris couldn't bring himself to read the rest. His blood ran cold, and his stomach lurched as he took in the attached picture of an attractive, smiling young woman with shoulder-length dark hair. His imagination overlaid that with the last picture of her in his head, and he dropped his phone on the table drawing the attention of his wife.

Without speaking he pushed the mobile toward her. She picked it up and scanned the article, paying closer attention to the details than he'd been able to stomach.

"Shit. Looks as though her family has reported her missing to the police."

Julie was frowning as she scrolled the article with one finger, before reading out the relevant part to him.

The missing person's team is aware, DI Anna Moore told us. "It's early days and our current line of inquiry is that Daisy may have stayed with a friend and neglected to tell her family her plans. If anyone has any information, we ask you to make contact with the police via our hotline or inform the family directly."

She sighed as she put the phone down and chewed her bottom lip in the way she often did when she was anxious or upset.

"What were we thinking?"

Julie whispered this as though to herself, but as she was looking right at him, Chris decided that she wanted a response.

"We weren't thinking Jules, that's the fucking problem. I think we should make an anonymous call to point the police in the right direction. At least her family will know what happened to her."

Julie's eyes filled with tears, but she shook her head vigorously.

"We can't Chris. If we do anything we risk it leading back to us."

Their eyes were drawn to the two black bin liners propped up against the backdoor, the rain had stopped during the night, and Julie stood up from the table.

"We still need to get rid of the clothes we were wearing last night."

Chris swallowed the lump that had settled in his throat. Julie had a point, they'd made their decision last night and now they had to be practical about it.

"We'd better get dressed first; the neighbours are going to think we're a bit odd if we start lighting bonfires in our dressing gowns."

Julie nodded her agreement. She was still biting her lip, her face pale and drawn, but Chris hardened his heart to her. She'd been the one to put the idea out there last night. She'd led the whole plan as far as he was concerned, in fact, the accident had been her fault more than his.

He flinched away as she laid a trembling hand on his shoulder. Turning his face from her hurt expression he marched out of the kitchen to throw on some clothes.

2

Chapter Two

DI Anna Moore hated this part of the job.

Although she had the outward appearance of not being affected, in reality, she had a kind heart that ached when she dealt with distraught relatives.

Mr. and Mrs. Landsbury had the stunned look familiar to those who had complacently believed that this sort of thing just happened to other people and not them.

Penny Landsbury, a well-rounded woman in her late 40s, had the grief-stricken expression that only the mother of a lost child would carry. Her husband, Jim, stood helplessly by her side, his greying dark hair sticking up in tufts.

Daisy was an only child, she worked at a local pub at night and during the day was attending college studying game design. Her parents described her as a responsible young woman. One who would never not let her parents know if she wasn't coming home.

In official terms, Daisy's case shouldn't have landed on her desk at all.

She wasn't classed as a vulnerable adult. There was nothing overtly suspicious about her disappearance, and no reason to suspect anything more than a young girl who'd neglected to update her parents that she was staying out overnight.

Anna wasn't sure why, but something about this case made her think there was more to it, and she wasn't one to ignore a gut feeling. The press had tried to link the case to Tilly Thorpe, but there wasn't a connection as far as anyone could tell. Tilly had been visiting her father miles away when she went missing and her case was in the hands of that local station.

So here she was, sitting in the Landsbury's kitchen sipping a coffee she hadn't really wanted but felt obliged to accept.

The longer she was here, listening to this devastated and frightened couple, the bigger her fears grew. This wasn't a girl who'd just disappear of her own accord, and Anna was becoming sure that she'd been right to override the usual process and open a file on Daisy.

"I'm going to need a list of all her friends. Was it unusual that she didn't tell you where she was going when she left the house yesterday?"

Jim nodded his head slowly, almost as though it hurt to move.

"I didn't take much notice at the time. We trust her you see, but looking back, yes it was odd. She usually says who she's meeting or where she's going."

"And she left at approximately 7 pm? That'll be about two hours before the storm came in."

Her father took this one too, Penny looked incapable of speaking, her face set and blank.

"That's right, give or take a few minutes."

Anna made a mental note to get the CCTV checked around the surrounding areas. Cameras were everywhere, even in this small rural community.

"Penny, could you help make that list for the officer?"

His wife turned her empty gaze to her husband. She looked like a woman on the edge, thought Lisa, it wouldn't take much to push her and then she'd tumble over into despair.

Jim looked away, but not before Anna saw his eyes fill with tears.

"I'll do the best I can love; her mum knows more about her social life than I do, but..."

He trailed off, leaving unspoken that she clearly wasn't capable of doing anything right now.

Jim pulled the notebook towards him and chewed the end of the pen as he concentrated his thoughts. He scribbled a few names, a frown creasing his brow, before tearing the sheet off and handing it to Anna.

"I know there's a few I can't think of, but they'll know each other and give you the other names I expect. The regulars at the Winton Arms and the landlord are worth talking to."

Anna nodded; she'd already planned on that being one of her stops today.

"What was she wearing last time you saw her?"

Jim looked desperately at his wife again but she just stared straight ahead lost in her own nightmare.

"I'm sorry officer, you must think I'm useless. I didn't take much notice of her outfit, she was a jeans and shirt type kid mostly. I do know she'd have been wearing her favourite sneakers. Light blue, that whatchacallit colour – baby blue. She nagged me to death until I coughed up the money to buy them for her."

Jim smiled indulgently, and Anna caught a glimpse of the father who was wound around his little girl's finger. It made her heart ache, especially when his face crumpled back into an expression of despair.

Taking the sheet of paper, she folded it and tucked it into her pocket, nodding to both parents as she took her leave. Part of her was grateful to be out of the oppressive atmosphere of the house as she took a deep gulp of fresh air.

The pub was half an hour away from opening time when Anna arrived.

A large, solidly built man was pushing a sack barrow into the pub. It was stacked high with packs of lager, so he was carefully navigating around any potential hazards and didn't immediately notice her appearance.

When she cleared her throat behind him at the doorway to the pub he spun around and in a practiced tone told her they weren't open yet.

Anna flipped out her warrant card, the man grunted in reply, and continued his journey behind the bar.

"I need to ask you about Daisy Landsbury, she worked bar here, didn't she? When did you last see her?"

The man looked up, his grey hair was buzz cut around his square head giving him the appearance of someone you didn't mess with, but when he spoke, she saw a flitter of sadness across his face.

"Aye love, Daisy was a good girl. She worked the bar, served tables, sorted the stock, and did anything that needed doing basically. They say these young 'uns are slackers, but our Daisy was a grafter."

Anna nodded; this was another picture of a responsible, reliable young woman whose disappearance was totally out of character.

"When did you last see her, Mr Fletcher?"

"Just call me Charlie, Miss. She popped in last night, early doors it was, wanting to pick up her wages a day early."

"Was that usual?"

Charlie shook his head, "No Miss. Daisy wasn't one to ask for her wages early, she knew we'd have them ready for her on the day they were due. She'd take her time collecting them as though she was embarrassed by doing it. Like I said, nice kid."

"How long was she here for? Did she get her money?"

Charlie took a moment to answer, he ripped open the polyethene covering the beer bottles and started stacking the fridge with them while he thought. Anna left him to it, some people needed processing time and she'd learned that the best way to get what she needed was to be patient.

"I didn't have the whole lot ready, but I sorted her with half, and she was pleased enough with it. Went bright pink when I handed it to her and stuttered out an apology as though she was ashamed to be asking. I told her, don't fret love, it's your money and I've no problem paying you."

He paused again while he considered the other part of her question.

"She must've been here for about two or three hours. We got busy with an early rush, and I didn't take much notice. I know one of the regulars bought her at least one drink."

Even Anna's patience was being tried by this point. Did she have to ask for the name of the regular or would Charlie realise its importance on his own?

"Kelvin Wright, that's who bought her the drinks. Youngster, but a bit older than Daisy mind you."

"How much older Charlie?"

This involved the landlord counting on his fingers and rolling his eyes to the ceiling as he worked it out.

"He's around thirty I think, so eight or nine years."

Anna made a mental note of the lad's name, she'd definitely want to speak to him, at the moment he was looking like one of the last people to see Daisy.

Charlie gave a deep, weary sigh and looked at the large clock on the yellow-stained wall opposite the bar. It was a traditional pub, with dark wood stools around the scratched oak bar, random tables scattered around, and a carpet with a pattern that had faded into something unrecognisable.

It was the sort of pub that Anna imagined let the regulars have a smoke indoors after hours when they had a lock-in. Not that she was bothered, it wasn't her remit to be chasing up stuff like that. Charlie had seen her eyes wandering around the décor, and he was clearly aware that the nicotine-stained nets and walls told their own story as he paused what he was doing waiting for her comment.

There wasn't one. She genuinely wasn't the least bit interested in what they got up here, she just wanted to find the missing girl.

It was as though an unspoken conversation had taken place and Charlie threw her a look of gratitude before gesturing at the clock.

"I'm pulling the bolts on the doors in five minutes little miss. Happy to fetch you an early drink though?"

Anna looked longingly at the optics and then the fridge. A vodka and tonic or white wine would go down well about now, she thought, before reluctantly opting for a plain tonic, lemon, and ice.

The landlord deftly threw her drink together before yanking back the bolts on the sturdy wooden front door. He'd barely stepped away when it swung back and several customers in workman's clothes swarmed through. Their loud banter stopped short when they saw her perched on a bar stool. The age-old problem where everyone could tell she was police from the first glance.

The now subdued bunch requested their drinks and took off to a table as far away from her as possible and Charlie shot her a look.

"You're not great for business Miss."

Anna shrugged; she was sorry that she was going to be a dampener on his early doors trade, but Daisy took priority.

She decided to give it forty minutes tops, if Kelvin didn't show she'd head over to his address instead.

In the end, she didn't have to wait that long. It was only ten minutes until the door clattered open and then banged shut. A tall, blonde man with broad shoulders and a narrow waist strode in, his glance around showed her that he was used to being center of attention.

His eye landed on her and his face lit up in a smile that didn't quite seem to hold the warmth it should. Clearly not as astute as the other customers she could see he hadn't made her as old bill.

He made a beeline for Anna who played her part, tossing her long blonde hair in an uncharacteristically girly move as she slightly widened her blue eyes.

It was exactly the reaction he was looking for. She could tell that by the self-satisfied look that settled on his handsome face. Pulling up a stool next to her, he leaned slightly into her personal space.

"Whatcha drinking love? I'll get you one in."

Anna smiled right in his face and then watched as his smug expression melted away when she flipped her warrant card at him.

Kelvin shrunk back on his stool; his face hardened into a look of deep dissatisfaction at the loss of the prey he thought he'd found. Anna found something about him unpleasantly uncomfortable, she certainly wouldn't want him talking to her daughter if she had one.

"You were with Daisy Landsbury last night. What time did she leave?"

Anna saw his eyes flitter to the side as he tried to work out how much of the truth he had to tell her, so she decided to clear things up for him.

"I already know she was drinking with you, what I need to know is when she left and was she on her own?"

Kelvin shifted uncomfortably on the stool

"I might have bought her a couple, she's a nice girl."

Anna tried not to sigh out loud, it was going to be like pulling teeth getting what she needed out of him.

"Kelvin let's be very clear. Daisy has gone missing and at the moment you're the last person we know to have seen her. If you don't want me making this an official chat at the station, I suggest you start to talk."

He shot her a look of pure disgust, clearly not a man who liked to be challenged by a woman, Lisa noted.

"She left a bit after 10pm I think, might've been later, I bought her maybe two drinks. Charlie gave her an envelope, I think it was her wages, and soon after she cleared off out."

"Was she alone when she left Kelvin, or did she perhaps say where she was going?"

The sly look settled on his face again and Anna found herself wishing she could go old school and smack his irritating head off the bar.

"I heard her on her phone, she was saying something about talking face to face, dunno who she was talking to though. Pretty thing she is so I guess it could've been a bloke."

Kelvin audibly breathed a sigh of relief as she slammed her glass down and stood up, but before she left, she turned to him. Leaning down so only he could hear her she spoke into his ear.

"I think we'd all be better off if you stuck to playing with women your own age Kelvin. I have a feeling Daisy's dad wouldn't be keen on your interest in his daughter."

The man blanched slightly, but before he looked away, she caught the pure rage on his face.

Deciding it was a case of "enough said" she beckoned Charlie over.

"Could you download the CCTV for me over the time period that Daisy was here last night please?"

He was about to walk away when she called him back over.

"What time did Kelvin leave the pub that night?"

Charlie rolled his eyes, "Always the last to leave and that night was no exception. Must've been gone midnight by the time I finally got him out the door and bolted up behind him."

Anna was interested to see that while Kelvin was making a show of not listening to them, he was almost twitching. She didn't think it left him with enough time to meet up with Daisy, but at the moment who knew?

She thanked Charlie, who nodded briskly. He was busy yanking hard on an ale pump, the glass he held filling with a dark brown liquid.

Throwing him a thank you, and ignoring Kelvin's cautious glance in her direction, she strode out of the pub.

That CCTV would be interesting, she thought, at the moment this was the last place Daisy had been seen and she'd like to know who she spoke to apart from that toe-rag Kelvin.

Even more than that she wanted to know where she went after she left and who she was meeting. It didn't seem to be in Daisy's nature to be secretive, but it looked as though she had something planned last night that she'd definitely wanted to keep to herself.

Chapter Three

Julie had dealt with her bag first or rather tried to.

The damp clothes and the still-wet ground meant that the fire had just smoldered rather than burst into flames. His wife was all for pouring lighter fluid on it and getting it going but he reminded her that the neighbours might think it was a bit odd that they were that desperate to burn something.

At that, Julie had glanced anxiously over at the fence that separated their garden from the nosy Brents.

Terry Brent, and his wife Rose, had lived in the same house for over forty years. They'd raised their children there and had hung on to it long since they'd grown up and moved out. Terry was okay, it was Rose that was the issue, she was constantly poking her nose over the fence and complaining.

She had this insidious way of doing it that got right up his nose. Like when she saw them wheeling the BBQ out of the shed on a sunny afternoon.

"Oh, are you having a BBQ?"

Obviously, thought Chris, but he'd just nodded.

"That's a shame, I'd wanted to put a wash out but I won't be able to if there'll be a load of smoke. You aren't having a lot of people over, are you?"

Julie had smiled, that one she did where it was clear she didn't mean it.

"Yep, quite a few actually. Loads of people from work and a couple of the neighbours."

Chris remembered how he'd had to look away to stop himself laughing. That was an obvious dig, and Rose's expression showed it hadn't gone unnoticed either.

The smile that had started at the memory dropped off his face as he returned to the present, and the task in hand. It was also a reminder that they didn't want Rose nosing about and then remembering her neighbours burning clothes at a later date.

Julie was already stuffing her things back into the bin liner, she looked around desperately for an answer and then settled her look on the shed.

"Let's shove the bags in there until it dries out enough to burn them."

Chris took a peek at the adjourning fence to make sure they weren't being watched, just in time to see Rose's face pop up over the top.

"Please say you aren't planning to light a bonfire. I was going to do a wash while it was dry, and I don't want it stinking of smoke."

Julie put on a tight smile that tugged her lips but didn't touch her eyes.

"No, we're not having a bonfire Mrs. Brent, just putting some old clothes and belongings in the shed."

Rose's sharp eyes took in the two black sacks.

"Not taking them to the charity shop? I always donate our old clothes. Not only are we helping those less fortunate but we're recycling them."

The pious look that accompanied her words ensured they got the message that she didn't think much of their wasteful attitude. Chris saw that Julie was struggling to hold the friendly look on her face, so he jumped in with an answer.

"They really are far too tatty to be dumping off at a charity shop Mrs. Brent, not fit for anything but burning or rags."

Rose hmphed but didn't say anything more. She gave the couple one last stern look as though sure they were up to something, before disappearing back behind the fence.

Julie held her finger to her lips to indicate he wasn't to say anything, she leaned in next to his ear and whispered.

"She's probably behind there, listening in."

It took every ounce of Chris's willpower to stop him from moving away from Julie, her closeness made his skin crawl. It reminded him of her leaning over that poor girl's body and searching her pockets for ID. He physically shuddered at the memory, something that his wife immediately noticed.

Julie shot him daggers before snatching up her bag of clothes and leaving him to carry his own to the shed.

Chris flung his bin liner in the corner; its impact disturbed the dust and cobwebs creating shiny motes that floated in front of his eyes and tickled his nose. He scowled at Julie, who was studiously ignoring him as she carefully tucked her bag up against the wall.

Sick of the sight of his wife and wanting to escape the claustrophobic atmosphere being near her created, he decided he'd go out for a bit. Just a walk down to the river and back, clear his head, and hopefully, it would stop him from picking a fight with Julie.

She narrowed her eyes when he announced his intention to go out, and he was ready with his excuses if she suddenly said she was coming with him.

Luckily, and maybe because she was sick of the sight of him too, she just shrugged as he put on his shoes.

Chris pulled the door closed behind him resisting the urge to slam it, he already felt lighter being out of the house. Feeling a shiver down his spine he turned and looked back. Julie's face was looking out of the living room window at him. Her eyes were hard and her expression steely as though weighing him up.

He forced himself to wave cheerily at her, partly so she didn't know how much she'd got to him, but also so that any watching neighbour would think there was nothing wrong.

The riverbank was saturated, and Chris cursed his decision to pick shoes that weren't especially waterproof. His socks were soaked through, and their cold dampness clung unpleasantly to his feet.

Other than that, his walk had definitely done the trick. His head felt clearer, and he was taking the opportunity to think about the whole situation without Julie breathing down his neck.

What had he been thinking? Surely facing up to a potential driving ban would've been better than this? They'd hidden that poor kid's body and now her parents must be going out of their minds.

Chris started to wonder what would happen if he went to the police now, told them everything that had happened, and threw himself on their mercy.

He imagined the details. Walking into the police station, and waiting for an officer to come and get him. Being interviewed and then charged, before hopefully being released on bail while he waited for the inevitable trial.

The thought of all of this made his heart race with fear, but what really scared him was the thought of the rest of it. The publicity would mean that everyone would find out, work, his neighbours, their friends, and family.

They'll all hate you. You'll be all over the internet.

He'd seen it before with similar cases. The increasingly nasty and threatening messages on social media, the disgust that everyone would feel when they found out what he'd done.

And why wouldn't they be disgusted? It was exactly how he felt about himself.

Chris felt his throat close up, and his eyes stung with tears at the thought of that young girl, rotting under a hedge while her family desperately looked for her. Lost in his own miserable world he didn't hear anyone approach until they spoke.

"Why hello there Chris. How's Julie? Is she still going to book club? I might be interested in joining up, maybe I can talk to her about it."

Agatha Cross, the nosy old bag from two doors up. Chris's heart sunk, he really wasn't in the mood for the non-stop local gossip that she'd be eager to share.

She was a short, rounded woman, her fleshy body forced into a tweed skirt and sensible brown pullover. Chris couldn't imagine she'd ever been anything but old and miserable. The expression "looks like she's licking piss off a thistle" sprung to mind as suiting her down to the ground.

"Hi Mrs Cross, we're both well thank you. Julie's been a little busy lately but I'll pass on your message about book club. How are you?"

It did make the cogs turn for him though. There was something behind her words that sounded like an insinuation rather than a casual inquiry.

Agatha's sharp eyes read his expression, and he knew she'd filed it away in her box of "Useful things to know about the neighbours."

"I'm fine thank you, Chris."

There was a moment of uncomfortable silence while Chris dug around for something else to say to her. Unable to come up with anything he was about to say his goodbyes and escape when she spoke again.

"Late one for you and Julie last night? Out partying, were you?"

There was an irritatingly smug look on Agatha's face that suggested she was making sure he knew she'd been watching them. Chris remembered the curtain twitch he'd seen; he'd thought it was Agatha at the time.

Making sure he set his expression to neutral he gave a casual shrug

"Just out for dinner Mrs Cross, what with the weather it took longer than usual to get home."

Maybe it was just his guilty conscience, but he was sure he saw a slyness in the narrowing of her eyes as though she didn't believe him.

"Yes, it was a terrible night, wasn't it? Did you hear about that young girl going missing? How awful for her parents, I expect she'll show up though. You know how selfish these youngsters are, she's probably off enjoying herself and not giving a second thought to the upset she's causing."

Pausing for a moment while she built up the suspense Agatha flicked out her tongue and licked her lips.

"Then there was that other girl, Tilly something or other. A bit younger but nowadays those girls are always acting older than they are. Asking for trouble if you ask me."

Chris found it hard to come up with a reply that didn't involve telling her to fuck off. The malicious spite and love of gossip oozed off her with every word. Agatha flicked him with an up-and-down glance as though dismissing the disgust she must see all over his face.

"Well, I must get on. I'm on my way to the shops, give my love to your Julie, and tell her I hope she'll let me know about joining her book club."

Chris managed a terse nod in her direction before giving her an abrupt goodbye. As she marched away in the opposite direction he watched her for a moment, his stomach twisted in anxious knots.

What was Julie up to on the nights she was due at book club, he wondered, and could finding out the answer give him the upper hand he needed?

When he got home Julie was banging around in the kitchen. At first, he thought she might be making them something to eat, but she soon relieved him of that idea. Walking into the room all he could see was half of her sticking out of the cupboard under the sink, and when she appeared it was with a handful of bottles and rags that she dumped on the worktop.

Putting her hands on her hips she jerked her chin at the items she'd just found.

"You'd best get out there and completely clean and polish the car. That way if there's any evidence, we'll have got rid of it."

Chris raised an eyebrow at her.

"I'll have got rid of it don't you mean?"

Julie raised her shoulders in a shrug

"It might look a bit weird if I was out there doing it, when do I ever clean the car?"

"Never a truer word spoken"

Chris had muttered it under his breath, but bat ears over there had picked it up and was glaring at him.

"I don't think we'll get into the distribution of chores around the house, you might come off worse."

He didn't bite, what was the point, he thought, she'd just hammer it home until he eventually gave up. Best to just give up at the first fence.

By now Julie was filling a bucket with hot soapy water, she threw a large, orange sponge on the top and handed it to him.

"What now?"

"No Chris let's wait until it's too dark to see what you're doing. Yes, now. And while you're doing that I'll go and burn those bloody clothes."

He clenched his fist and slowly exhaled in a bid to push back the rage that was starting to build. It always did with Julie, once the love of his life, she was now the bane of it.

Intentionally slopping some of the water on the kitchen floor as he marched outside laden down with car cleaning fluids, he took a petty delight in the look of irritation on her face.

It took the whole afternoon to go over it thoroughly.

Apart from a small dent in the front of the bonnet, and Chris was pretty sure that had been there before, there was nothing incriminating on the car. The only time he paused was when Julie bought him out a sandwich which she dumped on the wall wordlessly before leaving him to it.

"That's what I like to see, a man taking pride in keeping his vehicle clean."

The boomingly cheerful voice belonged to Marcus Pollock. He lived with his wife, Sarah, a few doors down. They were in their 30s and back when they first moved in him and Julie had met up with them for drinks a few times. That had tailed off as his marriage broke down, but they remained friendly enough with the couple.

Chris managed to put a welcoming smile on his face.

"How are you? How's Sarah?"

Marcus bounced on the balls of his feet, from his tracksuit and trainers Chris didn't have to be a detective to work out that he was on his way for his daily jog.

"All good, we'll have to get together for a drink soon, it's been forever."

Chris made a non-committal mumble that could have been taken as agreeing, but unclear enough that he wouldn't be held to it.

Marcus waved as he trotted off up the street, and Chris watched him go before turning back to his task. Having completed the clean, he carefully poured the now dirty water down the drain before rinsing out the bucket and lugging everything back indoors.

Julie was dressed to go out when he bumped into her coming down the stairs, and he could smell her favourite, and most expensive shampoo and shower gel.

"Going anywhere nice?"

Chris kept his tone casual as if he didn't give a shit. He was putting everything back in the under-the-sink cupboard, so she came through the kitchen to answer him.

"Just book club. Shouldn't be late back."

Keeping his face hidden so she didn't see his expression, he called back to her.

"What book are you lot reading? Anything good?"

Julie's voice took on a sharp edge of annoyance.

"You've never been interested before. A Ruth Rendell, it's alright but I'm not sure how much we'll have to say about it as it's only been a week and I haven't read any more than a couple of chapters."

Chris was almost impressed by how easily she lied, if it hadn't been for the tell-tale twitch next to her eye he'd never have sussed her. Deciding to add a little fuel to the fire he passed on Agatha's message.

"That reminds me, I saw Mrs Cross earlier. She's interested in joining your book club and wanted you to let her know how to go about it."

Julie sighed. She was aiming for casual irritation but that twitch was jumping so fast he was surprised it didn't leap out of her face at him.

"I can't see anyone wanting that nosy old busybody in our group. I'll put her off next time I see her, maybe tell her we read spicy romances or something."

He was tempted to call her on it, but that would merely be a short-term reward. Whatever she was up to she didn't want him to know about it, and he intended to find out exactly what it was.

4

Chapter Four

DI Anna Moore was currently sitting in the interview room of the station with three young girls. She'd exhausted any leads from the pub and much as she disliked young Kelvin his late leaving time currently made him the least likely suspect. The pub's CCTV hadn't shown anything else suspicious. Like most girls her age Daisy had been caught checking her phone constantly but that didn't mean anything on its own.

Now she was hoping that Daisy's friends could fill in the gaps.

Suzie Croft, tall with the willowy build of a potential model, and honey-blonde hair that tumbled down her shoulders in carefully styled curls. Wide blue eyes regarded Lisa with a mild curiosity hidden behind the door that a Gen Z closes on someone as old as Lisa.

Katie Williams was a short girl with bobbed auburn hair and a wide, open smile that made her green eyes flash with good humour. Then there was Leandra King, with her tightly curled dark hair and warm brown eyes, but also the most serious-faced of the group.

Anna had made sure they were comfortable; she'd provided drinks and snacks and opened up with as much casual chatter as she could muster.

Now it was time for the real questions to start.

"I know it feels uncomfortable talking about Daisy, and even sharing her secrets with me, but if we're going to find her, we need to know everything about her."

Anna saw that all eyes went to Leandra, demonstrating who was the leader of the pack, and it was she who took the lead in answering.

"Do you think something's happened to her?"

This was the first step, they wanted reassurance that if they spilled their secrets, it would at least be in a good cause.

"Yes, Leandra. It's out of character for Daisy not to be in touch, she's made no contact with her family. Have any of you heard from her?"

All three shook their heads, and Katie's pale face flushed red, with her pale complexion it was impossible to hide the blush that stained her cheeks. Anna made a note that Katie was the one to watch for evidence of a lie.

"If you haven't heard from her, and you're not covering for her, what is it that you're hiding? It might seem like I'm really, really, old but I was your age once and I can tell you're trying to keep a secret for your friend."

Anna was hoping that a bit of humour might build a relationship between her and at least one or more of the young people in front of her, but from their scornful expressions she hadn't hit the right note.

"Who says we're hiding anything? You make it sound like we've done something wrong. Should we be calling our parents to sit in with us?"

This was from Leandra again, her sour tone matching her stony expression.

"You haven't done anything wrong, I just need to find Daisy. Officially you're all adults, but if you'd feel more comfortable with your parents being here then that's fine. I can call them and then we can wait for them to come before carrying on."

Anna was sure that this was going to be the moment they all shut down on her. They'd sit there in silence waiting for their parents, and once they came they definitely wouldn't talk in front of them.

Much to her surprise though, Katie spoke up with an evident tremor in her voice.

"My dad'll go ballistic if I drag him down here, I'd rather just get this out of the way."

Looking around anxiously she leaned into the other two and whispered to them. Unfortunately for Katie, it wasn't a good room for secrets and Anna picked most of it up.

"Why shouldn't we tell her? It's not as if Daisy can say anything, it's her own fault for going off like this."

Suzie was the first to nod in agreement.

"I second that, both my parents will go nuts if they have to drag themselves down here to sit in with me because I'm keeping quiet."

Leandra shrugged, she seemed less concerned than the others about her parents being called, indeed it had been her idea.

Anna sighed, "So which one of you is going to actually spill the beans?"

In the end, it was Katie who made a start.

"Daisy was seeing someone, we think he was older, or married or something. She wouldn't tell us his name, said he'd be in the shi.. in trouble if anyone found out about them."

Anna hid a smile at the girl's attempt to correct her language.

"Did any of you have a clue who it might be?"

The girls looked at each other for a moment before Katie piped up again.

"Well, she wouldn't tell us, but we did give it some thought and came up with some suspects."

She paused, and the others both nodded which gave her the encouragement to continue.

"There was that creepy bloke from the pub where she worked, Kelvin something or other. She was always saying he kept buying her drinks and leering at her while she was working. We did wonder about her boss, the landlord, but he's well too old."

The girls had warmed to their theme now and Suzie jumped in with her suggestions.

"Don't forget Daisy did a bit of babysitting, maybe it was one of the dads? You read about that stuff all the time don't you?"

All three girls nodded sagely at this and Anna hid a smile. It was one of those stereotypical urban myths where the babysitter had a wild fling with the older man of the house.

"Could you tell me who she was babysitting for? Just so we can follow up with them."

Leandra appeared to have got over her reluctance and was eagerly joining in.

"A couple of her jobs were up on Oak Street 'cos it wasn't far from her road so she could walk up there and back. Mr and Mrs Wilk, they've got two kids Bobby and Carrie at number 6, and Mr and Mrs Harrow at number 35. They've just got the one, a daughter called Lottie."

Katie nudged her friend, her face was flushed again but this time Anna realised it was with the excitement of having more to add.

"Don't forget Mr A, he lives on Oak Street too, she used to clean around his house for him once a week. He lives on his own not married or nothing."

Suzie nodded, "Oh yeah, Mr Angel. He was one of our teachers at school. She saw an advert in the newsagent's window for a weekly cleaner and she took it on around her pub shifts. Can't see it being him though."

The girls all sat back expectantly, Anna could see they'd run out of names now and were waiting for her feedback on how helpful they'd been.

"Thanks, girls, I've got quite a few people to follow up on here. If anyone else occurs to you can you let me know?"

Anna passed her cards out, one for each, and was pleased to see they all carefully stashed it away. As they filed out of the room she looked at her list.

May as well pop up to Oak Street, if everyone's home I might get to talk to them all and see if anyone rings alarm bells.

Oak Street was one of those culdesacs that always reminded her of one of those weird shows where everyone was cloned. The houses were almost identical, each had at least one large and expensive car on the drive and the gardens were immaculate.

Her first stop was Mr. and Mrs Wilk at number 6. The car parked in the drive suggested at least one of them was home to speak to. Her ring on the doorbell was answered by a man in his mid-forties wearing shorts and a shirt. His bare foot tapped the floor impatiently as he waited to hear what she wanted with an irritated expression.

Anna flipped open her warrant card to show him as she introduced herself, his expression changed from irritation to puzzlement. This clearly wasn't a household that had much contact with the police on a regular basis.

"Are you Mr Wilk?"

The man nodded, "That's me, not sure how I can be of service to the police though?"

"I'm here about your babysitter, Daisy Landsbury."

Anna intentionally avoided the missing person part wanting to see what his reaction would be.

She wasn't disappointed. Mr Wilk's look of shock may have been fleeting but it wasn't so fast that she didn't catch it before he replaced it with a more neutral expression of mild curiosity.

"Goodness, what's the young lady been up to? Anything we should be concerned about in regards to leaving her alone with our children?"

Nice save, thought Anna, Mr Wilk was clearly a man who thought fast on his feet.

"Could I trouble you to speak inside please Mr Wilk? It's uncomfortably warm out here and I'd like to explain my visit in private."

The man's eyes darted from side to side around her as though checking for nosy neighbours. Spotting one twitching her nets further up the road he tutted and waved her in.

"Bloody Agatha Cross, nosy old cow. It'll be up and down the road in no time that I had a young female visitor while my wife was at work."

The glare he shot her suggested that he was holding her entirely responsible for the potential street gossip.

"Do you work from home, sir?"

Anna was taking in her surroundings, the living room that he'd taken her into seemed to be the main hub of the house. A rumpled blanket half covered the sofa and a bowl with dried-on milk suggested Mr Wilk hadn't long finished breakfast.

"Call me Paul, Mr. Wilk makes me sound more like my father. Yes, I do work from home, I'm a freelance illustrator. My wife, Leigh, works in a solicitor's office as a secretary. The children are with her mother for the day so I can work in peace."

DI Moore made a couple of notes in her book, Paul seemed a little more relaxed now they were on his home turf, but there was still an interesting edginess to him.

"Unfortunately, Daisy hasn't been home in a couple of days. Her parents are incredibly worried as I'm sure you'll appreciate so I'm doing a few inquiries to see if I can find out where she is."

Anna had thought that sharing her reason for being there might reassure Paul, but if anything he looked more worried than before.

"How awful for them. You don't think anything's happened to her do you?"

"I hope not Paul, it's more than likely she's with friends, but better to be certain than to not act and then find out later she was in trouble."

He nodded and there was an awkward silence for a moment as though Paul wasn't sure what to say.

"So, if you could tell me about Daisy that'd be really helpful. How long has she babysat for you, what do you know about her and when you last saw her."

"We'd had her babysitting for about a year, maybe a little more. Daisy was always reliable, the kids loved her, and because she lived nearby she could often help out on short notice."

Anna smiled politely, at least she hoped it was politely, she was very aware that what she considered a friendly expression often didn't come off that way.

"I've heard much the same from everyone so far. Daisy was reliable, not the sort to just up and go off without telling anyone. That being the case I'm even more concerned for her welfare."

Paul swallowed, Anna watched his adam's apple bob as he did, a vein throbbed next to his eye and he bounced his leg up and down nervously. Was he just worried about his babysitter, or was there more to it? Had she managed to come across the "mystery man" in Daisy's life already?

She hoped not, Paul wasn't an especially unattractive man but there was nothing so overwhelming about him that he'd be able to seduce a much younger woman. Well, in her opinion anyway, maybe Daisy had seen something in him that she was missing.

Since the storm the other night the weather had settled back to sunny and dry with a lovely cool breeze. Leaving her car parked up where it was she walked the short distance up the street to the Harrow household at number 35. A woman was on the drive trying to contain a small excitable girl who looked to be around 5 or 6.

"Please get in the car nicely Lottie, we need to get to the shops."

The car door was open but Lottie seemed determined not to be enticed inside and completely blanked her mother as she continued to run loops around the car. The woman, a short, blonde who looked to be in her forties was pointing at the car seat where she wanted Lottie to end up and hadn't noticed Anna approaching.

"I'm DI Moore, are you Mrs Harrow?"

The woman smiled pleasantly and nodded.

"That's me, although please call me Sue."

Sue called over to her disobedient child, "Lottie please don't kick those stones at the house you'll break a window."

Anna hid a grin as the child intentionally sent one last stone scuttling towards the house before turning around and replacing the game with seeing how many stones she could hit the garden with.

Sue sighed and looked about to reprimand her again before shrugging.

"Pick your battles, if I put an end to this one goodness what's she'll come up with next. Lottie's a ball of energy and can be a bit of a handful at times as you can see."

That bought the conversation nicely round to the reason for Anna's arrival on her drive.

"Sue, I've been told that a young woman called Daisy Landsbury babysits for Lottie?"

Anna put a question in her voice as though unsure if the information she'd been given was right. Sue's face lit up in a bigger smile.

"Oh yes, Daisy is a godsend. Somehow she knows just what to do with our Lottie, she adores Daisy. In fact, Daisy is due to sit with her again later this week."

Sue's face suddenly dropped into a look of concern as she put together the police visit with questions about her babysitter.

"Nothing's wrong is it?"

Anna waggled her hand from side to side.

"We're not sure is the answer to that. Daisy didn't go home the other night and she hasn't been seen since. As you can imagine her parents are beside themselves with worry and I'm trying to trace her last movements. When did you last see her?"

Sue looked thoughtful, "She last worked for us last week, but I think I saw her two nights ago. Just before that storm came in."

DI Moore felt a buzz of excitement.

"Whereabouts did you see her?"

Sue waved her hand vaguely around her at the street.

"Right here officer, I was driving home and as I turned into the road I caught a glimpse of someone walking along the pavement. It wasn't until I got closer that I noticed it was Daisy, I waved but I don't think she saw me."

"Did she look okay?"

Sue was about to nod when she changed her mind and shook her head.

"Actually I thought it looked like she'd been crying. It was just starting to rain a bit so it could've been that but I was sure I saw tears on her cheeks. I really wanted to stop and check she was okay.. but ..."

Anna waited until Sue continued, she looked a bit awkward and uncomfortable for the first time.

"This makes me sound selfish, I waved at her and when she didn't wave back I didn't bother trying again or stopping the car. I just wanted to get home before the rain got heavier to get my washing in. Now you're telling me she might be missing and I feel terrible."

"Hindsight is a wonderful thing Sue, you can't look back and wish you'd done differently. What you have done is step up and make sure that I know about it, that's a really big help in a case like this."

Sue blushed, this time with pleasure at the compliment which she tried to wave off with an embarrassed hand flap.

"Is there anything else you can tell me about Daisy? What's she like, does she do a good job for you?"

Sue nodded vigorously, "She's marvelous. Reliable, responsible, and level-headed. Little Lottie had a fall while she was with her once and cut her head. It bled loads like head wounds do, but Daisy didn't panic. She just calmly called the restaurant and let us know. We came straight home of course, but we needn't of worried, Daisy had cleaned her up, put a dressing on, and cleaned up the blood from the rug too. If her parents haven't heard from her then I'd agree they're right to be worried, she's not the sort of girl to just go off irresponsibly."

Again, Daisy was being described as the responsible sort, now for one of the more difficult questions.

"Does your husband get along with her as well as you do? Sometimes we find each person has a different view and maybe he wasn't as keen as you?"

Sue frowned for a moment and Anna hoped she wasn't offended or suspicious by her question.

"I wouldn't say Bill has really had much to do with her. He had a friend at his office who had a false allegation made against him by a young girl and as a result, Bill avoids being alone with Daisy. I keep telling him she's not like that but he always says "Better safe than sorry." I guess he's right, but it does mean I'm left to do all the organising, if it rains for example I won't drink when we're out so I can drop her off."

Anna handed her a card, she smiled and thanked Sue, but also wondered if her husband was so cautious because he had something to hide.

"I won't keep you, you've been most helpful, but I would appreciate it if you'd call me if there's anything else you can think of. I'll need to have a chat with your husband too, will he be home later?"

Sue shook her head, "He's away on a business trip to the states I'm afraid. That's why Daisy babysat for us last week, so we could have a night out before he went."

That seemed to confirm that Bill wasn't even in the country when Daisy went missing. Unless it turned out he'd fabricated a huge story about being in America it wasn't likely he was involved. Anna mentally crossed him off the list.

"Thanks, Sue, and if anything occurs to you just give me a call."

Sue agreed readily and after bidding Anna a quick farewell resumed trying to persuade her daughter to get into the car.

Next stop, Mr. Angel, she thought. Maybe it was her cynical side, but having an ex-pupil doing his cleaning, and an attractive female ex-pupil at that, piqued her interest.

As she strolled towards his house she noticed one of the residents watching her from his drive. The tall dark-haired man was standing next to his car, he'd been about to open the driver's side door when he spotted her. Stopping what he was doing he seemed very interested in keeping a careful watch on her activities.

Nosy neighbour, she thought wryly, it's not always the stereotypical older woman. Maybe he's the self-designated neighbourhood watch person. Anna pretended that she wasn't aware of his now very intent stare, the last thing she needed was to be pulled into a conversation about what she was here for.

She'd almost made it to her destination when the elderly woman who'd been watching her arrival at the first house appeared in front of her. Anna was tempted to try and just walk around her but the woman wasn't going to let her get off that easily.

"You're a police officer aren't you? Don't bother denying it, I can smell one a mile away."

Anna nodded and resisted the urge to sigh with irritation.

"I'm the neighbourhood watch lead and as such I need to know if there's something going on I should be aware of."

"Just a few routine inquires, nothing to be concerned about Mrs Cross."

The woman looked irritated that Anna knew her name.

"And you are?"

"DI Moore."

Agatha scrutinised her ID, pulling down her little wire-rimmed spectacles to do so before muttering under her breath as though annoyed.

"What brings a Detective Inspector to our quiet little culdesac?"

Anna shot her a tight smile, "As I said, just some general inquires."

Mrs. Cross showed no sign of moving out of the way as she planted her feet more firmly on the path.

"Is it that missing girl I read about? Do you think someone here has something to do with it?"

Anna continued to smile, she was very aware of how annoying it was, a fact confirmed by Agatha's scowl.

"I'd best be getting on Mrs Cross."

With that, Anna brushed past the older woman and stopping only to wave at her continued to Mr Angel's gate. Agatha's face was a picture of irritation and Anna took a childish pleasure in having thwarted her attempts to be nosy.

Tom Angel was standing on his porch by the time she pushed open the little wooden gate that gave access to the path through the front garden. He had his arms folded over his chest and a wary expression on his face. A thin sheen of sweat made his skin glow and his sports shorts looked damp as though she'd caught him mid-way through exercising. Anna gave him what she hoped was a reassuring smile.

"What did she want?"

He jerked his head towards the retreating back of Agatha Cross.

"She was telling me about her role as neighbourhood watch. I'm DI Moore."

Anna felt that was vague enough to put the subject to bed but Tom remained tense.

"What brings an officer of your rank to our quiet little street?"

Pointing at the doorway behind him Anna suggested that it might be better to take it indoors. Tom hesitated before shrugging and stepping back so she could go in.

There wasn't much of what her mum would've called "a woman's touch" about the place. Minimalistic and spotlessly clean, the bulk of the space in the living room was taken up by home gym equipment.

Tom popped the top on a bottle of water and gulped it back before holding the bottle against the back of his neck.

A stocky, muscular man that Anna could imagine he was the subject of many a teenage crush at school. In his own home and away from the prying eyes of Agatha Cross he seemed more relaxed as he invited her to take a seat on the pristine white sofa.

Anna cautiously sat down hoping that she didn't mark the seat, she was always uncomfortable in homes this perfect. She supposed it harked back to her childhood, she'd spent some time living with her paternal grandmother who'd been very rigid about cleanliness.

"So, DI Moore, what brings you to my door on this fine summer's day?"

There was something false about his flowery question that grated on her, and she noted that his upturned lips created a smile that didn't touch his eyes.

"I'm here about Daisy Landsbury, she hasn't been home for a couple of days and I've heard that she cleaned for you. Could you tell me the last time you saw her?"

Tom looked thoughtful for a moment as though working it out.

"We didn't have an exact day that she'd come each week, she worked at the local pub and did my cleaning around her regular shifts. The last time she was here working was last Thursday."

Anna wondered at the way he'd built up his answer and noted that he'd specifically said "when she was last working here" as opposed to when he last saw her. Deciding that she'd file it away and pick it up later she moved smoothly on.

"Is Daisy a good worker? Are you surprised that she'd go away without letting her parents know?"

He crossed his ankle over his knee and pulled the leg of his shorts down, but not before Anna got an unnecessary eyeful of more of him than she'd have liked to. Catching the smirk that tilted his lips briefly she put on her professional expression and waited for him to answer.

Seeing that he wasn't going to get the reaction he wanted Tom carried on as though nothing had happened.

"She was punctual and did what I asked of her. I'm sure someone has already mentioned that I was her teacher before she left school and in my experience, I'd say she was more responsible than most young people I've come across."

He shrugged, "Even the most reliable of us sometimes act impulsively or out of character. Who's to say she hasn't met some dashing young man and run away with him for a bit of fun?"

Anna nodded as she scribbled in her notebook as though he'd said something profound and not something that she'd already considered and was keeping in mind.

Once he was relaxed she threw in the question she'd been waiting to ask at the right moment.

"You said that the last time Daisy worked was last Thursday, but what I wanted to know was when you last saw her."

Tom Angel tensed up, his jaw hardened and his fingers flexed as the atmosphere in the room became uncomfortable. Anna flicked a glance towards the exit checking she could reach it unobstructed. It was a reflex move based on her experience as an officer. Suspects could turn in the blink of an eye if they thought you were on to them, and Tom suddenly appeared more hostile.

"Since she only comes to my home to work then it would stand to reason that I'd use the last time she was working to answer you wouldn't it?"

Again this wasn't really an answer just a diversionary question, but it did tell Anna more than Tom had intended. It told her that he was avoiding a direct answer, and in her experience that meant he had something to hide.

5

Chapter Five

When he'd seen that woman earlier he hadn't given it much thought at first, apart from an admiring glance. He'd assumed she was a salesperson, one of those door-to-door sorts who rang the bell and then blathered on about how they'd save the householder an absolute fortune on their internet bills.

Usually, it would've annoyed him to have one of those falsely bright cold callers on his doorstep, but he could do with a distraction, and since this one was attractive he was quite looking forward to letting her talk on about whatever it was she was selling.

Pretending to be digging in his pockets as though looking for his car keys Chris waited for her to walk up his drive after she'd left Sue Harrow chasing her hyperactive daughter around. However, instead of coming over to his house, the next logical one to call on, she seemed to be headed straight toward Tom Angel's place.

He was sure she'd clocked him looking but was intentionally pretending she hadn't. He watched closely for a moment, his hand hovering over the car door handle as though about to get in. She was definitely a woman on a mission. She knew which houses she wanted to visit, and that made him sure that she wasn't a salesperson after all.

If she wasn't sales, who was she?

Chris wondered if she was overthinking it, maybe he was just paranoid because of what had happened.

What do you mean by "because of what happened?"

The voice in his head was slightly mocking as it pushed him to name the deed. He pushed it away, using euphemisms gave him comfort, besides, it was his wife who should be the one feeling guilty.

He waited outside until he saw the woman ring Tom's doorbell before going inside.

Julie hadn't seemed overly concerned with his story about the strange woman visitor. She'd been distracted and brushed his suspicions away as though his words were annoying flies that needed swatting.

"I don't know why you're getting yourself so het up love. I heard at the shops earlier that it's common knowledge she had an older lover and they ran off together."

Chris felt the urge to slap her.

It was so strong that his hand actually twitched and he could see himself doing it. Lashing out and hitting her on the cheek with the flat of his palm leaving a bright red handprint behind.

If he'd thought it would work he might've gone ahead and done it, but he knew his Julie. She'd give as good as she got and it wouldn't end well for either of them to have the police called out for a domestic.

Instead, he gave her a withering look of disgust.

"That may well be the common gossip in town, but we both know differently don't we?"

He was rewarded by her blanching, her face lost some of its colour but her eyes flashed with anger.

"You're a prick Chris, was there any need for that? If you hadn't been drinking none of this would've happened, don't you go blaming it on me."

He felt his hands curl into fists and it took all of his willpower to unfurl them and keep his temper in check. Chris narrowed his eyes as he saw the smirk twitching on her lips.

"Much as I'd love to stand here having an in-depth conversation about your insecurities and paranoia, I've got bookclub."

The bounce in Julie's step as she walked away from him had annoyed him enough but then he heard her hum happily to herself as she closed the front door. There was no way she was this buoyant about sitting around and talking about a book with a bunch of people.

Book club my ass!

Chris decided to give her a headstart. Not long enough that she got away from him but just enough that he'd be able to tail her without being noticed.

He picked up his car keys and slipped out of the door. She'd have just reached the end of the road by now and if he hurried he'd see if she turned left towards the next town or right to the high street.

"I'm so glad I caught you, Chris."

He winced at the familiar voice of Agatha Cross, she was standing at his gate and waving at him as though he was an aircraft that needed guiding in.

"I was just on my way out Mrs Cross."

Keeping his head down he headed for his car hoping he'd be able to slip into the driver's seat and get away. No such luck.

"I won't take up much of your time. It's a neighbourhood watch issue and I'm trying to speak to everyone in the street."

Agatha positioned herself right in front of his car, so with a sigh, Chris resigned himself to having to hear her out.

"The police have been in the street today, apparently a young girl is missing and they seem very focused on our residents here."

Chris wondered if his irritation was making him paranoid because he was sure she shot him a sly look as though checking out his reaction to the news. He also felt a rush of triumph, paranoid was he? Wait until he told Julie that he'd been right to be concerned about the woman he'd seen earlier.

"Did she live around here then? I thought she was from the estate on the other side of the field?"

Chris felt his response was appropriately casual and patted himself on the back. Agatha eyed him like a spider in the corner of a web waiting to snatch up a fly.

"Maybe they think someone in the street knows something. We could be living right next to a murderer for all we know."

He felt his stomach twist, why would she say that? Everyone thought she was missing not dead.

"That's how rumours start Mrs. Cross, I'm sure we wouldn't want to make things harder for her family by spreading malicious gossip would we?"

He was rewarded by Agatha narrowing her eyes and glaring at him.

"Are you calling me a gossip Chris? How rude! I'm simply trying to keep this street safe and that policewoman wouldn't even give me the time of day. I've half a mind to complain to her superiors, we've got a right to know what's happening in our own street."

Her face was aglow with self-righteous indignation, but underneath he could tell she was trying to read his every reaction.

What did she see when she was twitching her curtains the night you came home after the accident? Has she been watching you ever since, and if so, what has she seen?

The voice in his head was making sense, had Agatha seen something suspicious? Was she sounding him out before she went to the police about him?

Agatha tapped her walking stick impatiently as she waited for him to answer and he felt his stomach flip over. He needed to get away from her before she pushed his buttons and he said something that made her even more suspicious. Glancing around he noticed a few of the other neighbours were outside, that teacher from over the road and that guy with the two noisy kids at the end of the culdesac. His friend Marcus was warming up for his daily jog and of course Rose Brent, the nosy cow from next door was leaning over her fence as though trying to hear what Agatha was saying.

"I'm sure we'll find out in due course Mrs Cross, anyway, I need to be getting back indoors."

He turned toward his house but her voice stopped him before he'd taken a step.

"I thought you were on your way out Chris?"

Letting his irritation show he shrugged, "Unfortunately we spent so much time talking that it's now too late and I'll have to rebook my meeting for tomorrow."

That's it, his voice congratulated him, let her think she's inconvenienced you. That'll explain why you were off with her.

Agatha smirked, "Oh dear what a shame, never mind, I'm sure whoever you were meeting will understand you were held up by important local business."

Deciding it was better not to answer her he rudely turned his back and stalked back into the house. His heart was racing as he twitched the curtain back to check she'd gone. At first, he was relieved to see Agatha was no longer planted on his driveway, but then he noticed she'd only moved one house up.

Rose Brent was waving her hands as she spoke and he quickly dropped the curtain back into place as both women looked over at his house.

Shit.

Was Rose telling Agatha about the aborted bonfire they'd tried to have the day after the accident? Were they putting together their suspicions with plans to go to the police?

That policewoman had looked as though she knew exactly who she wanted to talk to earlier. She hadn't gone door to door to speak to everyone and that suggested they had a lead they were chasing up. Was it a good sign that he wasn't on the list, or did it mean she was asking his neighbours about him?

Chris's hand shook as he poured himself a shot of rum and downed it one. His throat burned and his eyes watered at the taste of the neat spirit, but he ignored that and hastily refilled his glass. The alcohol was doing its job, calming his nerves and letting him think with a clarity he hadn't had earlier.

This was serious. He needed to talk to Julie and let her know, maybe between them, they could come up with a plan. Chris sank down on the sofa his glass of rum in one hand and the other clutching the bottle as though it was a comfort blanket.

The clock seemed to move slower than usual as he waited for Julie to come back. All thoughts of where she'd really been and confronting her were pushed aside and all he could think about was the humiliation of being arrested in front of his neighbours.

Two hours later he finally heard Julie's key in the door. The bottle of rum was now half empty and the alcohol buzz was keeping him from leaping at her the minute she walked through the door.

"Why on earth are you sitting here in the dark getting pissed on your own? For fucks sake Chris can't you manage a few hours without me here to hold your hand?"

Her spiteful voice penetrated the alcohol fog and he jumped to his feet. As he strode over to her he was rewarded by her flinching away from him and taking a step back.

Good, let her know who's boss in this house.

The voice in his head sounded smugly proud of itself so he ignored the sting of shame he felt. He'd never been a violent man, he despised men who intimidated women, and yet he suddenly realised how easy it was to become one.

"Don't fucking start Julie. I've been dealing with shit all day while you stick your head in the sand and pretend everything's fine. That woman I saw earlier was from the police. I've just had chapter and verse from Mrs Cross, who by the way was looking at me as though she suspects something's going on."

His outburst drained the colour from her face and he was pleased to hear a tremor in her voice when she spoke to him again.

"Are you sure?"

Chris let the silence hang uncomfortably for a moment letting her squirm.

"Of course, I'm bloody sure. What would the police be doing here unless they suspect someone in the street? She was probably asking all our neighbours about us and I bet it didn't take five minutes before Agatha was telling them what time we came home that night. Don't forget Rose, she saw us trying to burn our clothes the next morning."

Julie sank back onto the armchair behind her and pointed a shaky finger at the bottle.

"Got one in there for me?"

Chris was about to tell her to stick it and get her own fucking drink, but it was good to see her having to rely on him for a change so he grabbed a fresh glass and poured her a shot.

Julie gulped it back, coughing and spluttering at the unfamiliar burn of straight liquor the colour slowly came back to her face.

He poured her a top-up and after a second's hesitation splashed some more into his own empty glass too. Julie looked thoughtful as she tried to come up with a plan.

"We need to nip this in the bud, the question is, how?"

6

Chapter Six

Agatha carefully watched the milk in the pan to make sure it didn't boil over. Once it was hot enough she poured it into her mug and stirred in the chocolate powder and sugar. It was a little too warm tonight for hot chocolate but as it was part of her nightly routine she had it anyway.

Agatha sat by the window in her front room where she could see through the gap in the curtains into the street beyond. This was her watching point, the place where she could see what everyone was up to. She even had a notebook on the small table next to her chair so she could make notes if anything interesting came up.

Taking a sip of her hot chocolate she smiled to herself, this was the taste of her childhood. It reminded her of her mother, her careworn face and hands chapped by the chemicals she used at the laundry where she worked. No matter how tired her mum was or what time she'd got home she always made Agatha a hot chocolate before bed and plaited her hair into braids.

Her mother had been a good honest woman. Widowed during the war, and left to raise her small daughter alone on her widow's pension that she supplemented with the job at the laundry. Mavis had never complained, not even when she was crippled with arthritis and then diagnosed with terminal cancer that took her only three months later.

Goodness knows what she'd have thought of the goings on that Agatha saw day in and day out. Women who skulked around cheating on their husbands and children who did as they pleased without so much as a stern word from their parents. Tutting to herself she carefully noted down the interesting conversation she'd had with Rose Brent earlier.

Rose was a woman after her own heart. Principled and with strong moral values they often fell into conversation about the state of the world they'd found themselves in. She shook her head as she remembered trying to talk to Chris Knight outside his house.

The rude man, pretending he was on his way out and then making it clear he'd been lying to her by going back indoors instead of getting in the car. He summed up how his generation treated the one before them. No respect and acting as though the world owed him. His wife was no better either.

Agatha smiled again, but this time it wasn't the mists of nostalgia that pleased her, it was the thought of what she knew about Julie Knight.

There was nothing of interest out there tonight, thought Agatha with a pang of disappointment. Usually, there was at least a dog walker letting their pet foul the pavement and not picking it up to make a note on, but tonight even they hadn't been past her house.

As she drank the last of her hot chocolate she took one last look outside before plodding back to the kitchen. Placing her cup in the sink she filled it with water so the residue wouldn't stick to the sides before heading off to bed. Holding onto the banister as she made her way up she wondered at how quickly age catches you up. Once she'd have made short work of these steps but now she had to cling to the rail like a frightened child to keep her balance.

Agatha folded back the blanket and sheet before climbing in and getting comfortable. She looked at the empty left-hand side of the bed as she did every night and whispered goodnight to her Bert. He'd been gone fifteen years but she missed him every day. His photo smiled down at her from the wall where she could see him every morning when she woke up.

Sleep was drifting in just as Agatha heard something scratching downstairs. She frowned, I hope it isn't mice, she thought. Dealing with mice had always been Bert's job and it wasn't something she wanted to take on herself.

She'd just laid back on the pillows when she heard a sharp creak, that sounded like someone walking on that loose floorboard in the hall. Anxiety gripped her heart in a cold hand that made her shudder.

You read about break-ins but you never think it'll happen to you.

Agatha swung her legs out of bed and stuffed her swollen feet into a pair of fluffy slippers. Her arthritis was playing up tonight and every movement was painful. She wasn't sure what she was going to do, maybe if she could get to the phone she could call the police.

The problem was she'd refused to get one of those new-fangled mobile thingies so the only phone in the house was the landline on the hall table by the front door. The man who'd fitted it had offered to add another line up here but she'd refused. Who needed a phone in their bedroom, she'd asked with a laugh, he'd be wasting his time installing something so pointless.

Obviously, she was kicking herself now, but the choice had been made and she had to work with what she had. Agatha picked up a heavy vase from the hall. It was tall, bulky, and an alarming shade of green. She'd never liked it but Bert's mother had bought it for them as a wedding gift so she'd been obliged to display it. Even after his mother was gone Agatha had kept it out, somehow it wouldn't have felt right not to. Now she was grateful for that rare emotional decision as she felt the solid weight of it in her hands.

Holding on to the vase wasn't easy with her arthritic fingers curled almost fully over and it meant she couldn't grip the handrail on the way down the stairs either. Cautiously Agatha put her foot on the first step and gingerly put her weight on it while she bought her other foot down to meet it. One step at a time, she thought, that was the way to do it. Listening intently before daring to take another step she felt the vase start to slip out of her crooked fingers. She tightened her grip and swallowed to lubricate her dry mouth.

Fear wasn't a word that Agatha bandied around unnecessarily but tonight she readily admitted that she was afraid. With no idea who was down there and what they wanted, she was tempted to flee back to the safety of her room. She could hide under the sheets like a small, scared child who'd had a nightmare and stay there until morning bought the daylight.

Tempting as that thought was Agatha was made of stronger stuff, it wasn't in her nature to cower out of sight and run from confrontation. Determination renewed she carefully moved on to the next step, from here she could see right down into her hall. The phone sat tantalisingly within sight.

She could almost imagine picking up the receiver, pressing 9 three times, and hearing the calm, reassuring voice asking her, "What service do you require?"

"Police please," she'd whisper so the intruder didn't hear her.

This imagined conversation was enough to boost her confidence. She took a deep, steadying breath and lifted her foot to make the move one more step down. It was then that it happened, one foot in the air and the other half off of the step meaning she had even less balance than usual. The vase had finally become too much for her twisted hands and swollen joints to hold on to. Agatha tried to catch it before it hit the floor and gave her away, but as she reached out to it her knee gave way and she lost her footing.

The moment that her feet slipped out from under her was almost in slow motion, as though time itself was mocking her by letting her think she could rescue herself. The vase hit the step below her with a crash and she tumbled down behind it. Her crooked fingers clawed at the walls as she tried to find something to hang on to that would break her fall.

Over and over she tumbled, head bouncing from the wall to the steps as she rolled towards the hall. Agatha closed her eyes, she squeezed her lids down as tight as she could not wanting to see where she was heading.

Not being able to see meant she wasn't aware that she was going to smash into the hall table until she did. There was a moment of blinding pain, a flashing white light behind her eyes, and then it was all over.

Chapter Seven

Chris was still sleeping in the spare room. In fact, he'd moved so much of his stuff into it that he supposed it was no longer a spare room and just "his room."

Sleeping was another description that didn't quite fit either. He hadn't slept properly since the accident and spent hours laying on his back staring at the ceiling trying to unsee Daisy's pale face and staring blank eyes.

Tonight was no exception, but to add to his discomfort he had a cramp in his lower right leg. He couldn't get comfortable no matter how much he wriggled, shifted, or turned over. Sighing in annoyance he decided he might as well get up and find a book to read. Swinging his feet out of bed and putting his weight on his legs he found eased the cramp.

Not wanting to disturb Julie, he could do without hearing more of her bitching, he didn't put the lights on and instead felt his way down the corridor until he reached the end. A dim light glowed from the lamp in the hall and he could see that the master bedroom door was ajar.

Peeking in through the gap he expected to see Julie sprawled out across what was once their marital bed. He often looked in on her and felt a flare of rage at how she slept the sleep of the innocent. No tossing and turning for her as her conscience shouted out what she'd done.

Tonight however the bed was empty, the sheets rumpled and the pillow creased on her side showing she'd been there earlier and had then got up and left. Chris frowned, was he going to find her downstairs, sitting there waiting for him like a cat watching a mouse?

Not bothering to be quiet he stomped down the wooden staircase and ran his hand along the banister that he'd lovingly hand-sanded back to its former glory.

Poking his head around one door and then another he checked every room on the ground floor without finding Julie. Pouring himself a glass of water he sat at the breakfast bar while he drank it.

Had she really had the front to go off with her lover for a late-night rendevous? Slipping silently out of the house while her husband slept, did that shit give her an extra thrill?

Banging his glass back down on the counter he checked the hall, yes, her shoes were gone so she'd definitely gone out.
Fucking bitch.
Dirty, lying bitch.
Sneaking around and meeting up with whoever it was she was screwing.

Chris knew he wouldn't get any more sleep tonight, instead, he was going to wait right here for her. Let her slip into the house and then find him sitting there. See what bullshit excuse she came up with, or maybe she'd actually have the balls to tell him the truth for once.

Two coffees later he moved onto the rum and managed two more shots of that before he finally heard the front door creak open. Julie was obviously making an effort to come in quietly not knowing it was too late for that.

There was a quiet click as she closed it and he heard the muffled sound of her shoes being put back in their usual place. Her bare feet made hardly any sound as she tiptoed down the hall and he waited until he saw her figure at the bottom of the stairs before making his presence known.

"Where've you been?"

Julie jumped as though he'd stabbed her with a pin.

"I couldn't sleep so I thought I'd take a walk and see if that helped."

Chris snorted and shook his head at her.

"That's lame even by your low standards. Since when did you like taking midnight walks? Who is he, Julie? Is it someone I know?"

The scornful look she shot at him made him curl his lip in disgust, but she just laughed at his expression.

"That's paranoid shit Chris and deep down you know it."

"Oh no Julie, quite the opposite in fact, deep down I know that you're sleeping with someone else. God knows we haven't had relations in months, so who're you screwing Julie?"

His wife threw back her head and laughed.

"It's late and I'm going back to bed and I suggest you do the same. Talk to me again in the morning. Maybe you'll have realised how stupid you're being by then and we can stop this nonsense."

Chris watched as she ran up the stairs and heard the door to her room slam closed behind her. He knew she was up to something and most likely it was an affair. The problem is he needed unrefutable proof, evidence that she couldn't deny.

The next morning neither of them had got over last night's row. Julie slammed his coffee in front of him just avoiding slopping it over the sides.

Note to self, he thought, I probably need to start making my own coffee otherwise I'm going to end up with third-degree burns one of these days.

He shot her a look that she ignored, taking her own coffee to the chair that was furthest away from him she got her phone out and busied herself scrolling through it.

Chris usually thought she was just checking the news and her social media, but now he was wondering if she had the audacity to be messaging her lover right in front of him.

Feeling his eyes on her she looked up.

"What now? Stop gawking. I really can't be arsed with your paranoia shit at this time of the morning."

Chris didn't bother with a response, to him the fact that she'd raised it made her look more guilty not less.

As guilty as you both are over that poor girl's death? What's an affair compared to that?

The voice prodded at him souring his mood even more and just to top off his day when he threw his mug in the sink it hit a saucepan and the handle snapped off. It was his favourite mug too, the one he'd bought on holiday that always reminded him of long lazy days and sunshine.

"For fucks sake!"

Julie smirked at him, "Shouldn't throw things around like a sulky toddler then should you?"

Chris was so close to exploding he could feel the anger burning his guts. Turning away from her smug, irritating face he snatched up his keys and wallet. Glancing back at the kitchen he could see that she'd already stuck her nose back in her phone, a dreamy smile on her face as she tapped the buttons.

Going out the front door Chris nearly passed out when he saw the number of police cars across the road. That woman officer was there, but this time she was surrounded by uniformed police and white-suited forensic officers.

He watched in horror as they made their way in and out of Agatha Cross's house. Hearing a vehicle approaching he noticed the black coronors van drive up the street and park up outside the house too.

Chris walked briskly down his drive and made a show of opening his wheely bin and pretending to put something inside while watching the goings on from behind the lid.

"I heard Mrs Cross was found dead first thing this morning. I know she was getting on a bit but she always seemed in good health to me."

It was Marcus, dressed in his running gear and jogging on the spot right next to Chris. Before he could answer Julie marched out of the house and studiously ignoring Chris she waved at Marcus before jumping into her car and pulling away.

Chris felt a stab of suspicion, was it Marcus she was sleeping with? Surely not. Him and Sarah always seemed so tight he couldn't imagine him playing around on her.

You never know with people though do you Chris? How many of your neighbours would guess you're a murderer?

Pushing that thought away he tried to give Marcus a reassuring smile while casually seeing what else he knew.

"Any idea what happened? There's a lot of police over there for an accident."

Marcus shrugged, "I only know that someone told someone, who told my wife that Agatha was found dead."

Waving at Chris, Marcus took his leave, jogging away down the street where he carefully avoided getting too close to the group of police and forensic officers.

Chris watched him go and giving Agatha's house one last look he jogged inside. Pulling out his laptop he tried to immerse himself in work but after reading the same email four times without understanding the contents he snapped it shut again.

Deciding to get himself another coffee he was in the hall at the bottom of the stairs when he saw the shadowy figure outside his door. The figure knocked a few times and he felt his blood run cold.

Who was it? Was it the police? Had they found evidence that had led to him or Julie?

Chris ran up the stairs and flicked back the curtain in the master bedroom to see who was down there. It was that bloody policewoman again, he thought with irritation. He saw her head move and he stepped back hastily, hoping she hadn't seen him. She must've done, he realised, as she was now holding down his doorbell with an impatient finger. He couldn't ignore that sort of racket and if she had seen him at the window he'd look even more suspicious.

He looked around wondering what excuse he could use for not answering sooner, and spotting the bathroom door it came to him. He'd sling a towel around his waist and tell her he was having a shower when she'd knocked.

Since he'd stopped using the master bedroom the en-suite had become solely Julie's domain. This meant the big bath towel wasn't there as she tended to go and hang it in the airing cupboard to dry after her morning shower. Desperate to carry out his plan he snatched up the smaller towel hanging on the rail, stripped off his clothes, and wrapped it around his waist. It was only just big enough and he wasn't happy about the idea of opening the door like this.

No choice, he thought, just get it done, and maybe the more inappropriate you look the quicker you'll get rid of her.

Turning on the tap so he could splash some water on his hair to add that final touch he ran down the stairs to answer the door.

8

Chapter Eight

DI Moore decided she may as well do a few house-to-house inquires and start getting statements from Mrs. Cross's neighbours on if they'd seen or heard anything suspicious.

There wasn't anything to suggest that her death was anything more than a fall down the stairs by an older lady who was unsure on her feet at the best of times let alone at night. What was making Anna wonder if there was more to it was the coincidence of an unexpected death coming at the same time as her missing person case.

Heading for the house across the street she tapped on the door. There was no answer but she was sure she saw a flicker of movement as though someone was in the hall. Leaning forward to check she tapped again, but still no reply.

Anna stepped back and glanced up at the house as though it could tell her why no one was home. At that moment she saw the flicker of a curtain in the upstairs window and what looked like a face.

In her experience, the only people who avoided the police like that had something to hide. Pressing her finger against the doorbell she held it down long enough to be annoying. A few blasts of that she thought, and whoever was skulking about in there would soon decide it was better to answer the door.

Sure enough, she didn't have long to wait until the door was flung open. Anna stepped back, the man now standing on the threshold was wearing the smallest towel she'd ever seen around his waist. It just about fitted and the hem ended at the top of his thigh promising her yet another unwanted view of someone's privates if the wind blew the wrong way.

Flicking open her warrant card she introduced herself.

"DI Moore, I'm investigating the sudden death of one of your neighbours, and you are?"

The man stared at her for a moment as though she was speaking a foreign language and he had no idea what she'd just said. She was about to repeat herself when he finally answered.

"Chris Knight, I live here with my wife Julie."

Anna nodded and then gestured at his lack of attire.

"I'd rather speak when you're dressed sir. I don't mind waiting here while you put some trousers on."

He looked down at himself and blushed as he looked awkwardly at Anna and then at the door. It seemed as though he was now working out what to do. Leave her on the doorstep for all to see, or invite her in and then have her inside his house.

Anna waited patiently as decision made, he waved her inside.

"Wait here, I won't be a mo."

Mr Knight seemed to think he'd made it clear that Anna should wait for him in the hall but she decided against that idea and checked the doors until she found the one that led to the living room. After that strange game of hide and seek earlier and then answering the door to a female almost naked, she wanted to learn a bit more about this man.

The living room had a very definite woman's touch to it. Everything was coordinated nicely from the light grey sofa to the metal blue and cream scatter cushions on it. As she'd thought there were photos in frames on the surfaces and hung on the walls giving her the first glimpse of Julie.

Anna noticed with interest that there didn't seem to be many recent photos around.

"Can I get you a drink officer since you appear to making yourself at home?"

Ignoring the obvious dig she smiled at him, "No thank you, sir."

She pulled out her notebook and a pen and saw him glance anxiously at it. Chris was finally dressed appropriately in a pair of shorts and a baggy shirt with bare feet.

"Just a couple of questions that we're asking all the neighbours around here. How well did you know Agatha Cross sir?"

Chris shrugged, "Not that well, she stopped to talk to us once in a while. I don't want to speak ill of the dead but she was the local gossip and mostly we tried to avoid her."

Anna couldn't help but feel that he was hiding something. It wasn't anything she could put her finger on just a gut feeling.

"And were you and your wife both home last night?"

There was a hesitation before he answered her. It was a microsecond but Anna's instincts, honed by years of reading people picked it up.

"Yes, both of us were home last night."

"Anything that with hindsight might now seem to have been suspicious?"

Chris shot her a look, "Why? Do you think it was more than just an accident?"

Anna smiled, "I can't say, sir, our job is just to check everything and then put it together to try and make a full picture."

She tapped her pen on her pad in a way she hoped suggested she was still waiting for an answer.

"Nothing suspicious, not that we heard or saw anyway."

Anna nodded, snapped her pad closed, and tucked it into her bag along with the pen. Chris was watching her and she read his impatience to get her out of the house. There was also that strange behaviour earlier, and although his hair was damp the towel and the rest of him had been bone dry. If she didn't know better she'd think he'd just slung a dry towel around his waist, but why? Had he deliberately picked the smallest towel in the house, was that how he got his kicks?

Chris Knight and his wife were definitely getting run through the system along with the others she'd met on this street, which seemed full of some of the strangest people she'd met. Anna was about to head back to Agatha's house to see if there were any updates when the woman who lived next door to the Knights called her over.

"Officer, over here! Can I have a quick word please?"

An elderly lady stood at the end of her drive waving and beckoning Anna over. As soon as she had her attention she was in full swing.

"I'm Rose Brent, I live here with my husband Terry, I don't like to get involved if I don't have to but Agatha was my friend."

Anna hid her impatience, did this woman have something important to pass on or was she another one just looking for the gory details?

"I don't know if it's important or relevant but yesterday evening I saw Agatha talking to him next door, that Chris, and then afterwards she came over to speak to me. She was very upset, he was terribly rude to her, but then I'm not surprised, he's rude to everyone. Him and his wife are having problems apparently, although Agatha saw them come home after midnight the other night. It would've been the night they reckon that Daisy went missing, that's how Agatha knew which night it was."

Worth taking a note of, she thought, it wasn't much to go on but that guy had twanged her antenna earlier.

"Thank you, Mrs. Brent, that's really helpful, did Agatha tell you what they fell out about?"

"I don't know if it was so much a falling out as a disagreement. Agatha had gone over as part of her role as neighbourhood watch to tell him the police were in the street questioning people."

Rose threw an accusing look at Anna, "She was most put out that you lot wouldn't tell her what it was about."

Anna decided not to comment and wait for her to continue, with a disappointed expression Rose went back to her story.

"Anyway, Agatha said when he got there he was about to get in his car, the wife had left a few minutes before him. No idea why they couldn't go in the same vehicle, but that's the young 'uns for you, It's no wonder we've got this environmental malarky is it? Well, the way she told it was he was all put out at being delayed leaving, but when she left he didn't get in the car he just went back in his house."

Looking around like she was worried someone was listening in Rose leaned in towards Anna.

"Agatha said he looked very anxious, cut her off, and pretended he wasn't interested, but she reckoned his ears were standing up like a dog being called by its owner."

Rose was looking meaningfully at Anna's notebook, "Aren't you going to take notes?"

She obligingly scrawled a few lines but her mind was ticking over as she glanced up at the Knight's house. It'd be interesting to know if either of them had ever had any contact with Daisy before too.

Tom Angel's background check hadn't thrown up anything especially interesting. He'd moved to the area about eight years ago to take up a teaching job at the local secondary school. A school where Anna's niece Natasha was currently a pupil.

Anna had often found the most useful information didn't come from official sources. Bare bones, black-and-white information on previous offending, and parking tickets wouldn't tell who a person really was. The real insights came from those who knew them day to day, the people who knew things that would never be noted down or stored in a system.

Hence Anna was currently sitting in a coffee shop with Natasha having spent a small fortune on cream-topped coffees and overpriced cakes. Natasha was a good kid who had ambitions to join the force herself one day. She understood the need to keep their conversation just between them, but most of all she was very observant.

Tasha, as she preferred to be called, was dressed in her usual emo get-up of black everything, matched up with a pair of heavy duty DMs.

Before Anna could ask her anything Tasha jumped in with a question of her own.

"Is there any news on Tilly? I know it's not your case, but she was one of the few kids I could talk to from time to time."

Anna shook her head sadly, "Sorry love, I haven't heard anything, but as you say it's not even my case. So, would you be okay telling me about Mr. Angel."

"Mr Angel? Yeah, he's the PE teacher and a form teacher. Not mine, I've got Miss Wright thank goodness."

"Why thank goodness? Is Mr Angel not very popular then?"

Tasha shook her head, "Not at all. Actually, he's the most popular teacher at school it's just me that's not so keen on him."

Tasha went quiet and sipped at her coffee, wiping the cream from her upper lip with a napkin while she thought about what to say next.

"Aunty Anna, this is something I haven't told Mum. It wasn't anything really awful and I didn't want her making a fuss. Mr Angel is just so popular and if Mum went down there making a big deal out of it I'd end up getting shit off the other kids forever."

Anna didn't like the sound of this, and she certainly didn't want to promise to keep a secret that might turn out to be too big not to tell her sister about. She also didn't want her niece to clam up so she'd need to tread carefully.

"Tasha, I'll only tell your Mum if whatever you tell me puts you or someone else at risk, does that sound fair?"

After a moments thought the girl nodded her head, "Deal."

Tasha took a deep breath, "This is probably going to sound worse than it actually was. Anyway, I'd had to take a note to Mr. Angel's form room, I knocked and waited for him to say come in. His form had gone so he was there on his own marking books, I go over to the desk and hand him the note. He spins his chair around to face me and that's when I realise he's wearing really small shorts. I know he teaches games but I hadn't expected him to be dressed like that so I suppose I looked a bit surprised. He smiled at me and then rested his ankle on his knee. I don't know why I glanced down but I wished I hadn't because I could see, well, you know, more than I expected to."

Her niece was blushing by this point and Anna let her take a moment before asking her anything else. Interesting, she thought, exactly the same trick he played on me, but more disturbing when it's a teenage girl.

"Have you ever heard of him doing that with other girls at your school?"

Tasha shook her head, "Not that anyone would tell me, and most of the girls have got crushes on him so they'd probably like it anyway. It was just weird, when he saw I'd seen it he straightened his legs and gave me a look as though I'd done something wrong. The thing is I got the feeling he'd done it on purpose, but how do I prove that? If I say anything it'll look like I'm a silly kid with a crush who was perving at his legs."

Anna had to admit Tasha was right, men like Tom Angel could talk themselves out of most things. That sort of behaviour was a clever manipulation, it told him who was vulnerable and who to steer clear of.

It also made Anna wonder if there was anything more to discover about Mr Angel, he'd been local for the last eight years, but what about before that?

PC Chambers had spent the entire day watching CCTV for her. He'd isolated anything of interest and made notes on any sightings of interest.

"I've not found much footage of Daisy so far. It looks as though she left the pub around the time you've got her down for. I'd have thought if she was going home she'd head for the estate, but instead, she cut off into Palmer's field."

Anna looked at the still of Daisy leaving the high street, "That's your beat isn't it? What's your best guess on where she was heading?"

Chambers stared at the flickering image of what might be the last sighting of the young girl. His craggy face was full of sadness, it never got any easier when it was a kid or a youngster.

"I'd say there's two possible destinations. The kids off the estate like to hang around that field next to Palmer's, they burn out cars, drink illicit alcohol, and make out up there. Considering the sort of kid Daisy is, it's more likely she used it to get to Oak Street. It's a bit quicker that way, but it's also likely to have been boggy and difficult to navigate on a wet night. The only reason I can think of for her to use it would be to avoid being seen by anyone."

Anna tapped her fingers on the screen as though by touching it she could bring herself closer to Daisy.

"What were you up to?" She asked in a whisper.

Turning to Chambers she asked about the other footage she'd asked him to look for.

"What about that Kelvin lad from the pub? Any sign that he might have gone after her?"

Chambers shook his head, "I've got him leaving the pub just after midnight like the landlord said. He staggers up the high street and the cameras follow him back to his house. I've double-checked later and he doesn't come back out until morning."

That was Kelvin off the list, thought Anna. Shame really, the lad had definitely given off the wrong vibes.

"Any other faces of interest?"

"Not so far, but I'm going to keep looking for anyone else who takes that shortcut after Daisy does. I'll let you know if I come across anything marm."

"What about the checks on the names I gave you?"

His face said it all, nada.

"Sorry marm, all clean as a whistle. No history that would suggest they were involved. The only criminal record I found on Oak Street was a Chris Knight for a drink drive offence a few years ago."

Now that was a name that set off alarm bells. Maybe she was judging him too harshly by his weird behaviour and answering the door in a micro towel? Anna wasn't convinced, but a drink drive conviction hardly made him a master criminal.

He'd be one to watch though, and she'd keep his name on her people of interest list for now.

Chapter Nine

He'd watched from the window as the policewoman left and then his heart sank as he saw Rose Brent wave her over. They talked for a while and then he saw DI Moore look over at his house. What was that stupid woman telling her?

The police and forensic officers were in and out of the Cross house all day, he was drawn to the window all day and hardly got any work done because it was impossible to focus on it.

Chris pounced on Julie the moment she came in.

"That bloody policewoman was here today asking questions."

Julie's face paled, "What questions? Was she asking about that girl?"

"No, it was about Agatha Cross."

His wife's face relaxed as though that was good news.

"Thank goodness, you had me worried there for a minute. Silly old bag fell down the stairs, we should be grateful really. Every cloud has a silver lining and all that, now she's definitely not going to be causing us any problems."

Seeing his incredulous expression she laughed in his face.

"What's the bloody problem now Chris? I sometimes think you like to create issues where there aren't any."

He couldn't believe her audacity, first, she's dismissive about Agatha's death and a police visit and then she acts as though they've got nothing to be worried about.

"We killed a kid Julie, for fucks sake how can you be so blase?"

Narrowing her eyes at him she stepped forward into his space, Chris took an automatic step back not wanting her anywhere near him.

"YOU killed a kid Chris, not me. Let's get that straight from the start off shall we? And listen good, because that's the story the police will hear if all of this comes out on top. I'm not taking the blame or going to prison just because you're a useless, whining little shit who can't keep it together."

Clenching his fists he was finding it hard not to take a swing for her as she glared at him, hands on hips and spitting spite and bile at him. She must've read his expression because she started goading at him even more.

"Go on big man, why don't you have a pop and get it over with? You'd better make it count though because I'll come for you if you ever lay a finger on me."

It took all of his willpower to unclench his fists and step away from her but the thought of what she could do to him helped keep his temper in check. Her reaction also raised a few questions.

Had she really sneaked out to meet her lover last night as he'd assumed, or had she decided to silence Agatha Cross?

Julie could see she'd won, he could tell by the smug expression on her face and the way she was already looking around as though eager to leave the room. Now the thought had popped into his head he couldn't stop thinking about it.

"Anything else before I go upstairs for a well-deserved soak in the bath with a glass of wine?"

Chris opened his mouth to tell her about Rose and how the policewoman had spoken to her too, but then he stopped.

If Julie really did have anything to do with Agatha's death would he be signing Rose's own warrant if he said anything?

Julie snorted, "So that's the sum of your news is it? Great, thanks for the update. Not."

She turned her back and his gaze flittered to the heavy vase on the sideboard. Her stuck-up mother had bought it as a wedding gift and he'd always hated it.

Pick it up Chris, swing it back as far as you can, and smash it on her stupid, ugly head. Put a stop to this nightmare once and for all.

His hand twitched, it would be so easy. Maybe he could take her up the fields and stick her under the hedge with that poor girl. The living room door closed behind her and the opportunity passed, but Chris was still shaking with adrenaline.

He'd never felt so close to hurting anyone before, but Julie was starting to press all the wrong buttons.

10

Chapter Ten

Finding Tom's last teaching position had been more difficult than she'd thought it would be. Finally, pulling in every favour she'd ever been owed she managed to find out it was an exclusive private school called "The Grange." Tom had taught there for nearly six years before suddenly leaving halfway through a term. He didn't strike Anna as the sort of man who'd woken up one day and had an urge to be in the state school system so there must be more to it.

Her next problem was finding out what that something was. Private schools had a habit of closing their doors on anything unpleasant that might impact their income. How could Anna get around that and speak to the right person to find out what she needed to know?

In the end, it was her sister who came to her rescue. They'd met up for a drink and she'd found herself telling Lucy about the case, not everything, and certainly not about Tasha, but enough to feel better for sharing.

"I might be able to help actually. Pass me my phone."

Lucy had shot her a grin before tapping a contact and after a bit of small talk got round to the favour she needed before hanging up.

"Bingo, little sis to the rescue. Polly Cleaves is willing to meet you, she's not making any promises that she can tell you everything, but at least you're in with a chance."

Now Anna was sitting in a cafe with a bacon bap in front of her and a mug of coffee to wash it down with. Polly was already twenty minutes late and Anna was starting to wonder if she'd changed her mind when the door opened and a woman swept in.

Looking around as though trying to work out who she was meeting was another give away so Anna raised her hand and waved her over. They both introduced each other and insisted on first names. Polly looked anxious, her small oval face was crumpled with worry lines and she kept glancing at the other tables.

"Are you okay here or would you rather go somewhere more private?"

Polly shrugged her bony shoulders, "It's not the usual sort of place staff from the school would frequent but I really don't want anyone to see me talking to the police. I'd had a couple of wines last night and felt emboldened enough to agree to meet you but now I'm having second thoughts."

"Are you still employed there? Lucy was under the impression you'd left?"

Polly nodded but waited to answer until the waitress had taken her order.

"I did leave, it's a horrible, toxic place. My new job is much better, it's a lovely place to work, but I don't want to risk them finding out and getting me fired. You wouldn't believe the reach and influence that place has."

Anna didn't say but she had a good idea, whenever a private school showed up in a case everyone knew they'd use their contacts to stop any awkward questions being asked.

"If you really feel it's too much of a risk to talk I'll completely understand."

Anna crossed her fingers under the table. She was hoping that her words would reassure Polly enough to loosen her tongue, if she said she couldn't then it was back to the drawing board. Polly twiddled her spoon around her coffee cup and picked a blueberry out of her muffin.

"Lucy's always been there for me and I owe her this much at least. Go on, fire away."

Anna felt a wave of relief, "Did you ever work with a colleague called Tom Angel?"

Polly's already pasty face went even whiter at his name and she clenched the coffee cup so hard Anna thought she was going to snap the handle off.

"What's he done? I should've guessed it'd be about him."

"He hasn't done anything that I know of, but I'm looking into a missing girl and his name cropped up."

Polly drew in a shaky breath, "I'm not entirely surprised, is he still teaching? It's not to do with that fourteen-year-old that went missing is it?"

Anna answered her questions one at a time, "Yes he's still teaching, at the local comp actually, and no, I'm not involved in Tilly Thorpe's case."

Polly went quiet again for a moment, "I'd hoped he'd given up teaching. He did say he was going to start up a business as a personal trainer after he left under a cloud."

She paused as though still unsure if she should be saying any more.

"So, the cloud he left under. The head was approached by one of the girl's parents who claimed Tom was having a relationship with their daughter, Stephanie. Mrs Hatt, the head, called him straight into the office, but he denied it completely. When the parents followed up on why he hadn't got the boot they went garrity. That was when they showed Mrs Hatt indisputable proof. Apparently, the silly girl had logged everything in her diary and kept every inappropriate message they'd sent each other. Even Tom couldn't talk his way out of that one. The parents were threatening to go to the police and Mrs Hatt persuaded them to drop it if she promised he was gone with immediate effect."

Anna sighed, she'd been expecting as much, but it didn't make it any easier to hear.

"So, he just left without a fuss?"

Polly nodded, "He didn't have much choice really, not with that sort of evidence in front of him. He was always brash and bullish, but not even Tom could make up a story to excuse that lot away. There were threats to report him but he swore he was giving up teaching so Mrs Hatt let it go."

Anna pushed away the ball of anger burning her stomach like acid. Deals like this led to abusers like Tom Angel being able to carry on accessing vulnerable victims. If he'd been reported as he should've been then he'd never be working in a school now.

Polly looked nervous again, "I expect you'll want to speak to Mrs Hatt now? Is there any chance you can leave my name out of it?"

Anna nodded firmly, "It'll be as though you and me never spoke Polly, I appreciate your candor and I'll keep you out of it."

Mrs Hatt peered over her glasses at Anna.

It was a move that she assumed intimidated every child and young person it was aimed at, but it didn't wash with DI Moore. In her career, she'd faced down people way more scary than the headmistress of a posh school.

Her warrant card had easily got her past the woman's PA. Mostly because Anna had "accidentally" picked a time when she knew prospective parents were going to be visiting. She'd counted on the school not wanting her presence putting off the wealthy and influential families and she'd been right. The flustered PA had swept her anxious gaze across her open warrant card and had immediately buzzed her through.

Mrs Hatt wasn't as impressed though, her stony expression suggested that she felt above the law and saw this visit as an unnecessary inconvenience.

"I have no idea what brings the police to my office DI Moore. Does your superintendent know you're here? I have his personal number and it won't take me five minutes to check you out."

Anna had also faced way more scary threats than this one. Someone telling tales to her senior officer couldn't compare to hissed warnings that there was a price on her head.

"You're welcome to do so Mrs Hatt, there's no subterfuge here. I have a missing person's case and I need to check the background of someone who came up in relation to that case."

The headmistress looked as though she was weighing up her options, finally deciding that it would be simpler to deal with it than to make the call.

"FIne. I still can't see how anyone involved in something potentially criminal would be attached to our establishment, but go ahead."

Mrs Hatt waved her hand at Anna dismissively, but her smug expression dropped when she heard what, or rather whom, Anna was interested in.

"Tom Angel was a teacher here wasn't he?"

Dropping small amounts of information at a time had often served Anna well. The person she was questioning would be kept on edge never knowing quite how much Anna really knew.

Mrs Hatt fiddled with the gold-plated pen she'd laid down when Anna had come into her office earlier.

"I can't see how I can help you, Mr Angel is no longer a member of our staff team."

Clever answer, Anna thought wryly, but still not quite good enough to get her off the hook.

"I'm aware of that Mrs Hatt, I'm looking into the reason he left. When a potentially criminal matter isn't reported to the police we have to look at if there's a safeguarding concern."

Mrs Hatt narrowed her eyes, "This does not concern the police, it was an internal incident and was handled as such. We safeguarded our pupils and managed it with the sensitivity it required."

Anna was starting to feel irritated by her evasive answers and decided it was time to be blunter.

"Look, Mrs Hatt, your corporate speak isn't going to dig you out of this hole. Mr. Angel was accused of sexually inappropriate behaviour with a minor. This matter should've been referred to the police to investigate fully but it wasn't. To compound this dereliction of duty of care your school then saw fit to sweep it under the carpet so he was free to seek employment in another school. If it came to light that you neglected to safeguard other children using the legal framework set out for schools how do you think prospective parents would feel about entrusting their beloved offspring to this establishment?"

Mrs Hatt looked furious, but under the anger was definitely a growing tinge of fear, Anna noted with satisfaction.

"Someone must've been sharing confidential information for you to be aware of this DI Moore. All of our staff sign NDAs when they start work and these cover them after they leave us as well. If I find the person responsible I will be informing the board so they can take legal action."

Anna sent up a quick prayer that she could keep Polly out of it. She hadn't known about the NDA, no wonder the woman had been so nervous. Mrs Hatt gave an annoyed sigh before using the intercom to speak to her PA.

"Fetch me the Angel folder and the Harrington investigation please."

Eyeing Anna with a look that suggested she'd like nothing better than to turf her out of her office Mrs Hatt sat in silence until her PA rushed in and handed her the folders she'd asked for.

Flicking them open she scanned the contents before handing them both to Anna.

"You may not make copies of anything in these, and once read they will be returned to Gertie at the front desk. Gertie will allocate you a place to sit. You will not roam around my school or speak to anyone apart from myself or my PA. Is that clear?"

Anna hid a grin at her use of the teacher addressing a naughty student tone and nodded her agreement. She picked her battles and as she'd won this one she was happy to let Mrs Hatt have a small moment of superiority to salve her ego.

Besides, she now had the full name of the girl involved in the allegations, Stephanie Harrington.

Chapter Eleven

When Julie announced she was going shopping Chris couldn't help but wonder what she was really up to. He might've been tempted to believe her if it wasn't for the large number of red flags that suggested she was lying again.

The first was when she didn't pick up the car keys, she just grabbed a bag for life and started towards the front door.

"Not driving?"

Turning around and pulling a face at his question she sighed in exasperation.

"No Chris, I'm not taking the car. It's a nice day for a walk and we don't need much."

She sounded like an irritated parent talking to a persistently annoying child, overly patient as though humouring him.

"I thought we did a big shop the other day? Have we run out of basics already?"

He tried to sound casual but she narrowed her eyes and huffed a breath in his direction.

"For christ's sake Chris what are you implying? I forgot a few things so I'm going to pop out and get them. What's your problem?"

Without bothering to wait for an answer she stormed out of the door and slammed it behind her. Chris looked at the door thoughtfully for a moment before picking up the coffee cups and putting them in the sink. As he turned around his arm got entangled with something hanging off the back of the chair.

Yanking away he looked down in annoyance and red flag number two waved itself in his face. Julie's handbag, her day-to-day bag that she took everywhere. Chris frowned, it didn't mean she hadn't taken her purse, maybe she'd just got that out of the bag and taken it with her on its own. Not her usual behaviour but who's to say that's not what she did?

Open it, Chris, have a look and see for yourself. I bet it's in there, maybe you just don't want to know for sure?

He eyed the bag, it was tempting but he'd never violated his wife's privacy like this before.

Stop procrastinating and open the bag, if you don't check you'll never know. Do you want to carry on being kept in the dark?

His hand shook as he unzipped the top. Just a quick peek, he told himself, just quick enough to see if her purse was sitting in there. The zip sounded overly loud in the silent kitchen, rasping against the metal teeth until it got stuck on a stray piece of leather. He didn't want to tug it and risk causing damage that Julie would notice later so he carefully wiggled the zip back and forth until he'd freed it from the material. Now it moved freely, but the top of the open bag hung together as though trying to hide its contents from his prying eyes.

Chris peeled back the edges so he could see inside, realising that he'd need to put his hand in he pulled the bag closer. He didn't have to move much out of the way to see it, Julie's purse was virtually on the top, and under it was her mobile phone.

Heart pounding with fear and guilt at what he was about to do he pulled the phone out. He knew the passcode, they both knew how to get into each other's phones. Red flag number three soon waved it's brightly coloured self when he discovered she'd changed the code on her phone.

Why do that unless she's got something to hide? What's on her phone that she doesn't want you to see?

The voice sounded outraged on his behalf, and Chris felt his stomach churn with the betrayal he was facing.

Lying, cheating bitch.

Picking up his keys and phone Chris pulled on his shoes and headed out of the door. Julie hadn't got far, he spotted her just up the street, bag for life in one hand while the other waved expressively as she talked to Marcus.

He was wearing his obligatory jogging clothes and having just got back from his daily run was also coated in a sheen of sweat. Leaning against a post as he stretched his leg muscles Chris was sure he caught Julie shooting an appreciative glance at Marcus's bulging calves.

There was nothing overtly obvious, but he sensed an intimacy in how close they stood. Julie's body language certainly suggested she was being flirtatious, flicking her hair back and touching his arm when she laughed at his jokes.

Moving on down the street she stopped for a chat with Paul Wilks from further up the road. It was a shorter conversation than the one she'd had with Marcus, but no less suspicious. He hadn't even realised she knew Paul to speak to.

If she really was going to town for some shopping she'd now continue along the street and out onto the main road. It was still possible that she hadn't even realised she'd forgotten her purse and Chris was desperately trying to give her the benefit of the doubt.

Instead, Julie crossed over and after a hurried look around her as though not wanting to be observed scuttled towards that teacher's house. Chris had always found him to be unfriendly and any attempts at conversation had been short-lived and uncomfortable. He couldn't even remember the bloke's name.

He had to be careful not to be spotted and Julie suddenly seemed more aware of her surroundings. Slipping behind parked cars he hunched over so she wouldn't see him following her. Leaning around he just caught a glimpse of her leaning over the teacher's gate to speak to him when a voice from behind him made him spin round.

"What on earth are you doing?"

Rose Brent, nosy neighbour from hell, was staring at him with a look of incredulous disbelief. Thinking fast Chris tugged on his laces before standing up.

"I'm doing up my laces Mrs Brent. Have you not seen anyone tie their shoes before?"

Her gaze dropped to his feet, but far from accepting his explanation, she looked even more suspicious.

"Strange place to stop, if I didn't know any better I'd think you were skulking around spying on people. I hope that's not what you're doing."

Chris gritted his teeth, bloody annoying woman.

"If anyone is creeping about watching everyone I'd suggest it's the person who crept up on me just now."

Rose's face went as red as the flower she was named after. Unable to find a response she satisfied herself with a humph as she marched away back towards her house. Chris immediately looked over at the teacher's place only to find no one was standing outside.

Had Julie gone in or carried on her way? He couldn't see her anywhere and had once again lost sight of his quarry because of a nosy old bag. Sighing to himself he headed home. It wasn't over, he was going to find out what she was up to and with who if it was the last thing he did.

Julie came back about half an hour later, her face was flushed and she was slightly out of breath. Placing the empty bag for life on the table she announced brightly that she'd got all the way into town before realising that she'd forgotten her purse.

"What an idiot! So I ran all the way back and now I can't be bothered to go out again. It wasn't anything too important, I'll leave it until later or tomorrow."

Chris bit back what he wanted to say. He wanted to spit in her face and call her a liar, but showing his hand too soon wasn't going to get him what he needed. If he accused her now without any actual evidence she'd deny it and twist it around until it was all his fault.

Julie, however, appeared to be in the mood for a row because when that didn't provoke him enough she started in with more digs.

"It's the silent treatment is it? More paranoid thoughts about me cheating on you or claims that the elderly neighbours are spying on us? You need help you do."

She's winding you up Chris, don't bite.

The voice wasn't powerful enough to override his instinctive retaliation though.

"Don't bother gaslighting me honey, I know exactly what you're up to. As for the neighbours, it's lucky one of us is aware of what's going on. That nosy bitch next door is constantly showing up all over the place, you should be just as worried as I am about it."

Julie scowled at him, "Gaslighting, for fucks sake. Don't be a prick Chris, and Rose has always been a nosy bitch so what makes you think it's any worse than usual?"

By now his temper had simmered and he was regretting being so hasty in biting back. He needed her to just carry on with her deception otherwise he'd never catch her out, and as for Rose, well he couldn't take the risk after what happened to Agatha.

Deciding that ignoring her was the best option he opened his phone and made a show of scrolling through his news feed. He knew she'd feel as though she'd won this round and as predicted the tension in the room faded into relief that he wasn't going to question her further.

As Julie stalked out of the room with the air of a woman who'd got away with murder, he started to wonder if she actually had.

Chapter Twelve

Forensics were looking to move out of Agatha's house. Anna had kept them there as long as she possibly could, but now they were making noises about more pressing cases. Her gut feeling was that Agatha had something in her house that had got her killed, that or she knew something, or the killer just thought she knew something maybe?

Anna's other problem was that no one but her saw it as a potentially suspicious death. Nothing in the house seemed to suggest that anyone apart from Agatha had been there. When Anna pointed out that she'd been carrying a heavy vase when she fell the forensic lead, Teddy Balfour, had shrugged.

"I'm not saying she didn't think there was someone in the house, I'm saying I can't find any evidence that there was. I've got a bunch of fingerprints to check through. Most, if not all of them, will probably turn out to belong to the householder, but we live in hope."

Parking up a short distance from the Cross house she had to walk past Tom Angel's to get there. The man himself must've looked out to see who'd pulled up because she'd barely taken a step when he appeared at the end of his drive.

His face was flushed and she noticed he was clenching and unclenching his fists as he waited for her to get closer. Anna was tempted to cross the road to avoid him but why give him the satisfaction?

"I want a word with you DI Moore."

The hostility in his voice matched his body language and Anna prepared herself for an unpleasant confrontation of some description. As soon as she got close enough to hear him without him being overheard by anyone else he hissed his complaint at her.

"You've been poking around in things that are none of your business and if you don't stop I'm going to report you to your boss for harassment."

Someone must've filled him in on her visit to the school where he previously worked, Anna guessed.

"Mr Angel, can I suggest you calm down, please? I'm simply doing my job and ensuring I follow all and any leads that come my way."

She hadn't thought it was possible for him to colour up even more, but his face went an even darker red. His tensed neck showcased how muscular he was, and his broad chest, flat abs, and bulging biceps made her aware of how easily he could do her physical harm if he wanted to. Anna casually tucked her hand into her pocket as she adjusted her stance slightly so she was ready to move quickly if she had to.

Anyone watching wouldn't have seen what she was doing, but Anna was preparing herself. In her extra deep pocket was her retractable baton and feeling it's solid presence under her fingers was enough to give her confidence.

"My life is not a fucking lead officer. That little bitch made up stories and lost me my job and now you're raking it all up again."

Anna put on an expression that suggested she was interested in hearing his side of the story. If he was in the mood to have his say then she'd be listening and taking note of every word.

"I can see what you really think, no smoke without fire and all of that bollocks. Well, it wasn't true, not a damn word of it. She had a silly schoolgirl crush on me and when I tried to let her down gently and professionally she went running to her parents with that ridiculous story. They of course believed her, I can't blame them, but when the head took their side too, I was outraged."

He still looked outraged she thought. Was it the genuine anger of a wrongly accused teacher, or was he playing the role of one? Staying silent she let him vent, even his denials would give her more to go on.

"If you leave without a fuss Mr Angel no more will be said on the matter. And wouldn't it be better if you found a role that didn't put you at risk like this again."

His impersonation of Mrs Hatt was pretty accurate and she could imagine her saying exactly that. This time, however, she decided to risk throwing in an observation of her own.

"And yet you did continue teaching Mr Angel."

He stepped forward into her personal space and she gripped her baton ready to react if he spilled over into physical violence.

"Why the hell shouldn't I? It's my job and I don't see why I should have to give it up over a bunch of lies. If the school gets to hear of this I could be out of a job again. Have you thought about that? The damage you people do when you go tramping about in things that don't concern you?"

Anna waved her free hand in a calm-down gesture, "I'm sorry this has caused you so much distress sir but I must ask you to step back and stop raising your voice to me."

As though realising how close he was to her Tom made a noticeable effort to control his anger before stepping away. Anna allowed her hand on the baton to relax slightly but made sure she could still grab it quickly if he flipped out again. Luckily he appeared to have decided it was futile to threaten a police officer so publically, instead, he satisfied himself by glaring at her.

"There's no point even discussing it with you. All of you lot are the same. Uneducated, small-minded, and unable to see beyond the obvious."

"All of which lot are "all the same" Mr. Angel? Women? Police? Any particular group you're aiming that at?"

He smirked glad that his jibe had got under her skin as it was clearly intended to.

"You make your own mind up DI Moore. If the cap fits, wear it."

With that last rejoiner, he spun on his heel and strode back into the house leaving Anna to wonder what he'd meant by it.

As Anna pulled up outside the milkshake bar that Polly had insisted was the in hang out of the girls in Stephanie's year she wondered if she was pushing it too far. Daisy's case wasn't even officially considered serious and yet here she was pressing the buttons of the wealthy and influential. A matter that she was sure would be brought to her superintendent's attention at some point.

In for a penny, in for a pound, she thought as she pushed open the door and heard the old-fashioned bell announce her arrival. Stephanie and her friends weren't hard to spot, they were the only group of teenagers in the bar. Four girls all took up a booth in the corner slurping noisily from brightly coloured shakes. When Anna arrived next to their table they all looked up and she flicked her warrant card open.

"I'm DI Moore. Which one of you girls is Stephanie Harrington?"

The girl in question didn't need to answer. She went bright pink as the other three turned to look at her. Anna directed her attention at her as well and Stephanie looked down at the table top in embarrassment.

She was the smallest of the four girls. Short and slim wearing oversized clothes that dwarfed her tiny frame. Long blonde hair hung over her face and Anna noticed she didn't give off an air of confidence like her friends.

"What have you done Stephanie? You'll lose your position as the good girl of the group."

The teasing was good-natured, but Stephanie looked as though she was wishing the ground would open up and swallow her.

"Miss Harrington, would you mind if we found someplace more private to talk?"

Stephanie looked both grateful to have an excuse to escape and afraid of what it was that Anna wanted. Once they'd found a quiet table where the stares of the other girls wouldn't reach them Stephanie slid into the booth and fidgeted uncomfortably.

Anna had been expecting a girl who was more brash, and bolder, but instead, she'd found this wilting flower of a girl who looked afraid of her own shadow. She might be wrong, but she couldn't imagine her making up stories about affairs with a teacher.

"I can see you're anxious Stephanie. Please don't worry you aren't in any trouble. I just need to talk to you about what happened with Mr. Angel."

At the horrified expression on the girl's face, Anna tried to give her a reassuring look.

"Honestly Stephanie, no one knows I'm here. I just need to hear from you what went on."

"Call me Steph, only my parents and the school use Stephanie."

Her voice was small and timid, but it was a start, at least she was starting to open up.

"In your own time Steph, there's no rush."

The girl flicked her a look. Her big blue eyes looked too large for her small, oval face. She pulled the sleeves down on the jumper that must've been far too warm for the weather they were having and started pulling threads off the already ragged edges.

"Mr Angel was my form teacher and he took the boys for games. At first, he was really nice, he knew I was shy and he encouraged me to speak up. I liked the way he made me feel noticed. Mostly no one sees me, but he did. It was alright when it was just about school work, but then he started to get more personal."

Steph trailed off and Anna could see the misery etched in her face. This didn't seem like a kid who'd benefited in any way from disclosing let alone made-up stories.

"How did he get personal Steph?"

The girl coloured up again. Her pale face splotched pink as she looked for the words to explain.

"First he started complimenting me on how I looked, just casually. "You look lovely today Miss Harrington." Then he started staring at me in class and looking away when he saw I'd noticed. When I asked if I'd done anything wrong he blushed as though embarrassed I'd caught him. "Sorry Miss Harrington, I just can't seem to help myself." That was when I started to feel really uncomfortable, but he was one of the most popular teachers. The other girls would cut their right arms off to have him look at them like that."

Anna spoke gently, Steph looked as though she might leap up and make a run for it if she was pushed too hard.

"Was that when you went to your parents?"

Steph shook her head, "No DI Moore, I didn't tell them then. I just tried to wear different clothes and sit at the back where he wouldn't notice me as much. It was something else that made me tell."

The pause went on for a while and Anna was about to prompt her again when Steph started talking. She looked at a point over Anna's shoulder as though afraid to meet her eye.

"He asked me to stay back one morning and when I got to his desk I realised he was wearing shorts. Not the usual ones he had on for games lessons, these were too small for him and the leg bits didn't come down very far."

Steph was blushing furiously at this point and Anna felt her heart go out to the girl. She hated this part of her job. Making victims relive what had happened and then having to fight to be believed against a perpetrator who had the charm and confidence to make them look like liars.

"He sort of crossed his legs. You know when a guy puts his ankle on his knee and when he did his shorts rode up even higher and I saw..I saw..you know... his *thing*."

Steph looked as though she was going to burst into tears. Anna didn't need to ask her what she meant because she knew. Oh yes, she knew alright, she'd seen it for herself. This was also looking like a pattern of behaviour where he had a victim type.

"You did exactly the right thing Steph by telling your parents. This isn't something that any woman should just put up with. Men like Mr

Angel play on your insecurities and we have to be strong if we're going to stand up to them."

Steph managed a watery smile at her speech, and a little more colour stained her pale cheeks.

"You sound just like my mum, she said much the same as you. That was before she announced she was going to take some sharp shears and make sure he didn't do it again."

Anna grinned, "I'll pretend I didn't hear that!"

Feeling confident that she'd left the girl in as good a place as possible she urged her to rejoin her friends and thanked her for her help. Not wanting to hang around the shake bar and risk making Steph uncomfortable Anna left and returned to her car.

Sitting in the driver's seat, her hands shaking with anger, she replayed that poor kid's face in her head. The problem was he'd perfected his play. He could innocently pretend it was just an accident. "How embarrassing, I am sorry." Put in the right way it would seem like an unfortunate incident. Worst-case scenario he might get told to dress more appropriately, but nothing would happen that would stop him from doing it again.

She was still sitting there pondering how to deal with Tom Angel when her phone buzzed with a message. The Super wanted her back at the station – NOW.

Anna sighed, what fuckwittery was that about? Complaints from the posh school probably, she thought with annoyance.

Starting the engine she headed back to the station.

13

Chapter Thirteen

Chris was starting to feel as though Rose was some omnipresent thing in his life. Everywhere he looked he seemed to see her sour face staring back at him.

She peered over the fence when he was in the back garden, stood on her drive staring when he was in the front and twitched her curtains back as he walked by her house. It was getting to the point where he wasn't sure what was paranoia and what was real anymore. He'd hear footsteps behind him but when he'd turn around to look there was no one there. Chris was sure it was Rose, but what he wasn't so sure of, was why.

Did she suspect something or was she just losing the plot?

It all came to a head for him when he was sitting in the local pub trying to enjoy a quiet pint and saw her sitting with her husband at a table close by. Terry's full attention was on his pint, but Rose's drink sat ignored as she focused entirely on him. Chris had tried to ignore her. He'd got his phone out and attempted to concentrate on reading a book on his app, but her eyes bored holes in him.

In the end, he'd downed the rest of his drink and headed home. So much for having a break from sharing a house with a woman who he'd happily like to throttle. Letting himself in his annoyance boiled into anger when Julie shot him a look like he was an intruder in his own home. She'd been on the phone but hung up the moment she was aware of his presence.

"Don't bother on my account. If you want to whisper sweet nothings to whoever you're screwing just get on with it, pretend I'm not here."

Julie stormed over and waved the phone in his face, too close for him to actually see anything.

"I was talking to my sister actually. Not that I should have to explain myself to you. You're fucking paranoid, that's what you are, banging on about me having an affair. I think you're just covering for yourself. Maybe it's you that's playing away?"

Chris tried to snatch the phone out of her hand so he could see the proof for himself but she was too quick for him and yanked it out of reach. Wanting to frighten her into being less spiteful he told her about Rose before he could think it through.

Big Mistake. Huge.

Julie stared at him for a moment before laughing loudly in his face.

"You really have lost the plot, haven't you? The cheese has slid right off your cracker."

Twisting a finger into the side of her head in case he didn't get the drift.

You could make her stop if you wanted to. It'd be so easy Chris, it
    wouldn't take much. Strangle her. Snap her neck. Stick a cushion
    over her face.

Chris felt his hands reach out towards her and pulled them back before she noticed. Julie was far too busy mocking him to notice anything. Sticking her feet into her sneakers she picked up her keys and pushed past him to the front door.

"I'm going out, I need a walk and to be away from your madness so don't bother following me. Yes, I do know that you're creeping around like some crazy stalker."

He clearly hadn't been as careful as he'd thought. No wonder he hadn't caught her at anything, she'd been aware he was there the whole time. Looking out of the window he watched as she strode confidently down the drive and onto the pavement.

Chris was about to turn away when he saw her head next door. Craning his neck so he could see what was going on he soon noticed that Rose was standing at the end of her drive. Julie went over and Chris watched as the two women fell into conversation.

To him, it looked as though Julie had made the first move but he couldn't be sure. God, he hoped she wasn't confronting the woman about what he'd said. Rose would make his life a living hell if Julie told her Chris thought she was spying on him.

Julie was waving her hands expressively as she spoke and it looked as though she was smiling. Was she mocking him? Laughing at him with their neighbour?

Rose wasn't saying a lot but she was nodding her head as though agreeing before waving goodbye to his wife and heading back inside. Julie kept walking and he watched as once again she crossed the road, but this time she didn't go to that teacher's place.

This time she stopped and stared across the street at Agatha Cross's house, and it gave Chris a chill to see the small smile on her face.

Julie didn't stand there for long before she turned back and headed towards the house. Not wanting to be caught watching her Chris jumped away and took himself into the kitchen.

When he heard the front door open and close he waited until she came into the room before casually asking her about Rose.

"Saw you chatting away to Rose just now."

Julie shook her head despairingly, "Another paranoid accusation on its way is it? I knew I should've stayed out longer. She wanted to know about joining the book club if you must know."

Chris almost dropped the glass he'd pulled out of the cupboard to get himself a drink. Now he knew she was lying. Even if there was such a thing as book club he couldn't see her inviting Rose to join it.

She's setting the stage ready for when it all comes out. She's not going to take the fall, she'll make sure it's you who takes full responsibility.

I bet she was dripping poison about you in Rose's ear.

Chris glanced in Julie's direction, she was sitting at the table tapping out a message on her phone and studiously ignoring him.

Look how unconcerned she is, that's because she's laying the groundwork. She'll play the victim Chris and you'll be the monster.

There'd be evidence, he thought, evidence that linked them both and not just him. Plus she'd burned all the clothes they'd worn that night.

Are you sure she burned yours as well? Have you checked? You were busy washing the evidence off the car, maybe she just dealt with her own clothes and yours are sat in the shed waiting to be found.

He caught a breath as he thought of how it'd play out. The police smashing through the door and searching the house and shed. They'd appear with a black bag and he'd catch a glimpse of Julie's smug face before the cuffs were slapped on.

There was only one thing for it. Next time he was home alone he needed to check the shed, and if he found out she'd been setting him up....Well, he'd just have to deal with her.

14

Chapter Fourteen

Superintendent Young waved her into the seat opposite him.

A tall man with a long face that always looked miserable even when he was laughing, but he looked especially grim today. Anna sat and waited to hear the worst, if he was this pissed off it probably was that snotty cow Mrs Hatt who'd complained about her.

"DI Moore, I had a call from my counterpart across the border. Apparently, they have no evidence that Tilly Thorpe ever made it over to them. This means they're able to pass it back to us, like a gift that no one wants. Because we thought they were dealing with it we've now lost vital time and the trail will be stone cold. That aside, DI Moore, I need you to drop everything and get straight on this. It's got to be your priority, nothing else gets in the way of solving this. Her parents are devastated and the press are hounding everyone. Once they find out it's our case they'll be on our arses like flies on shit."

Anna rubbed her nose thoughtfully, this meant Daisy was supposed to take a backseat.

"What about the Daisy Landsbury case sir? I'm sure I can investigate them in tandem without either being neglected."

"Daisy Landsbury is an adult, she isn't vulnerable and she isn't a child. That means that she's not a priority DI Moore, is that clear?"

Anna nodded, she wasn't going to push it because the way he'd just worded it meant he hadn't strictly said no to holding onto the case.

"Crystal sir. Have they sent over their files so I can see where they got up to? No point going over the same ground if it can be avoided."

The Super seemed satisfied that she'd taken his orders on board and pushed a large folder towards her.

"I've forwarded it electronically as well, but I know how you prefer a hard copy too. I'll leave it with you Anna, try and get a result as soon as possible."

This was clearly a dismissal. Anna stood up and with a nod in the Super's direction headed back to her office.

Her desk was piled high with paperwork and slips alerting her to calls she'd missed while she was out of the office. Scooping them all up in a pile she shuffled through them, no one of interest. Stuffing them into her drawer she pushed the paperwork aside to make room for her new file.

Tilly Thorpe had left her mum's house after tea with her rucksack, she'd told her she was going to her dad's for the weekend. Her parents were divorced and Tilly was used to making the journey between their homes. She caught two buses and walked a short distance on the other side to her father's place.

When she didn't arrive her father had put off calling his ex-wife for as long as possible. It'd been an acrimonious divorce, he'd had an affair and she was still bitter. Reading further into the notes it appeared that Tilly had been caught out on other occasions telling her mum she was at her dad's when she wanted to do something her mum wouldn't have let her do.

With the parents reluctant to speak to each other Tilly got away with it more often than not and Anna wondered if she'd been planning to do the same thing this time. Maybe something had happened before she had a chance to contact her dad and cancel out.

The question was, what was Tilly up to that she didn't want her parents to know about?

Having once been a teenage girl herself Anna knew exactly who to ask, if Tilly confided in anyone it'd be her friends. With all the kids on summer break, Anna was going to have to approach each one at their home with anxious parents hovering nearby. Nothing put a teenager off from talking more than a parent listening in, so Anna was going to need to think about how to get what she needed.

There was one other person she was going to have to speak to. Tom Angel was her form tutor and Anna was pretty sure he wouldn't be pleased to see her again. Not that it bothered her to piss him off, but it wasn't exactly the way to get anything useful out of him. Thinking hard she suddenly smiled, DS Bridges was exactly the man for the task. If anyone could play to Angel's predilections and get to the truth of it, it was Nevile.

Tasha had proved invaluable once again.

Her niece knew exactly where Tilly's friends hung out, which apparently was the library. When Anna had given her a puzzled frown Tasha had shrugged and explained they were "readers."

"Basically it's just Tilly and one other girl, Belinda, they hang out at the library and compare how many books they've read over the summer."

Who was Anna to argue? Besides, kids who sat in libraries reading books didn't usually end up getting into bother, although that theory had fallen down for Tilly. The town library was a small, red brick building with a pitched roof that leaked when it rained. The council was as hit by cutbacks as the rest of the country and one of the "luxury" fundings that had been pared back to the bone was the library.

Mrs Hathaway had been the librarian for years. Anna remembered her formidable presence ruling the roost in her own youth. Memory loss clearly wasn't an issue for her either as on seeing Anna approach the desk she'd pulled down her glasses and recognised her immediately.

"Ahh Miss Moore, how good to see you. You were once a regular visitor and yet I think it's been more than a few years since I last had the pleasure."

Anna had been a bookworm at school too. With a family that struggled financially, the library had been a lifeline for providing her with as many books as she could read. Nowadays it was a different story, she earned enough to afford to buy as many books as she wanted. A whole room in her house was covered in shelves. Wall-to-wall books made it her favourite place to be on her days off.

"Hi Mrs. Hathaway, I'm more of a book buyer than a borrower these days! I don't know if you heard but I'm in the police now? Anyway, I'm looking for a young lady called Belinda, used to hang around with Tilly Thorpe?"

Mrs Hathaway smiled proudly at the woman she'd known nearly all her life.

"I did hear, well done you! All that studying paid off, I thought it would. Belinda is in her usual spot at the back next to the Thriller collection."

Anna tipped her a wink as a thank you, and felt a little choked at Mrs Hathaway's kind words. Her family hadn't been very supportive at all, not of her studying or when she decided to join the police. Her father had given her the up-and-down look of a man sizing her up before telling her that she was a disappointment to him.

Her mother hadn't been much better, but she made allowances for her. Veronica Moore had spent her entire marriage being bullied, downtrodden, and beaten by the man she'd married. Kevin Moore was a loud, brash man who'd broken his young wife and hoped to do the same with his daughter. The disappointment he felt had started the day she was born instead of the son he'd been expecting, and he'd never forgiven either of them.

Kevin Moore had died in a pub brawl five years ago. He'd picked a drunken fight with a man he'd thought he could easily beat. A mistake that had cost him his life when it turned out his adversary was a featherweight boxer. Anna had gone to the funeral, she hadn't wanted to and then decided it was best to make sure he was really gone.

It was too late for her mum though, too many years of being downtrodden and bullied had left her a shell of a person. Anna saw her when she could, but if she was honest she found it so difficult and depressing she didn't go as often as she should.

Shaking off the miserable trip down memory lane, Anna found herself standing next to a curvy teenager with mousy brown hair and a serious expression that showed she was immersed in her book. She cleared her throat and the girl looked up with an irritated expression that made Anna hide a smile. No one liked being interrupted when they were reading!

"Are you Belinda?"

The girl gave her an intense stare before nodding.

"I assume you're the police and you'd like to talk about Tilly?"

There was something about Belinda's forthright approach that endeared her to Anna. It wasn't often in her line of work that she met anyone who was honest let alone to the point of bluntness, so it made a refreshing change.

"At least there's no need to flick open my warrant card, I'm DI Anna Moore, and yes, this is about Tilly."

Belinda's face dropped and she sighed sadly.

"I know I come across as unfeeling, but it's been awful since Tilly vanished. It's not like her DI Moore, she's responsible and I just can't see her doing anything silly."

Almost word for word it was the way Daisy had been described too. For Anna, it was too much of a coincidence that two girls of a similar nature had gone walkabouts in her small town.

"Can you think of anything you can tell me that might help us find her? Anything at all, no matter how small it might seem to you."

Belinda looked down at her book, she wasn't reading it but Anna could see looking at the words comforted her. Finally, she raised her head and looked the DI in the eye.

"This isn't something I know for sure, but I strongly suspect Tilly was seeing someone. I don't know who they are because she denied it when I asked her, but she used to blush really easily and I knew when she was lying to me."

The young girl looked miserably down at the table, her shoulders hunched over as though she wished she could hide behind them.

"We fell out over it. I told her I knew she was lying to me and that she wasn't much of a friend if she didn't trust me enough to tell the truth. That was just before she went missing, I'd asked if we could meet up later and she said she was going to her dad's. I could tell she was lying, she used that as an excuse whenever she wanted to get away from her parents for the weekend."

Anna nodded, she'd thought as much, but what secret was so big that Tilly didn't tell her best friend?

"What did she usually do on the weekends when her parents didn't know where she was?"

Belinda managed a watery smile, "It sounds more exciting than it really was. Tilly used to come to mine, hang out, and read, nothing more wild than that. She found the whole thing with her folks really difficult, her mum had a new boyfriend and she didn't like him very much."

That was interesting, thought Anna, her mum hadn't mentioned a boyfriend to the police last time she was interviewed. Definitely a new lead to pick up on when she caught up with Mrs. Thorpe.

"Is there anything else you can think of that might help Belinda? Had everything been okay at school? I know you guys are going back soon and maybe she was worried about it."

Belinda blushed and shrugged as though dismissing the question. It was the first time Anna had felt the girl pull away and she wondered why.

"That's not an answer Belinda. I'm sorry to put you on the spot and I know you're trying to be loyal to your friend, but you really need to help us find her."

Belinda kicked the table leg a few times with her soft-fronted sneakers. It made barely a sound but the girl still looked around as though expecting to be told to be quiet.

"If anything Tilly was excited about going back, she was in Mr. Angel's form, and like most of the girls she had a massive crush on him."

"What about you Belinda? Did you like Mr. Angel as well?"

Belinda sniffed, "Not especially. I thought he was a creep, we fell out about that too."

Anna's ears pricked up, was this another victim of Mr Angel's shorts trick? She fit the victimology.

"Any particular reason you thought he was a creep, Belinda?"

The girl looked a little uncomfortable but she did look Anna in the eye as she answered.

"I don't suppose anyone will believe me, but he does this weird thing with his shorts where he lets them ride up so high you can see the tip of his penis. He did it to me once, but I just pointed at it and asked him to pull his shorts down lower. He gave me a filthy look and told me I was a dirty little girl for looking at him."

"Did you tell anyone?"

Belinda shook her head, "No way. Mr. Angel's too popular for anyone to believe he's a pervert. He's had it in for me ever since that day, I told Tilly, and I think from her reaction he did it to her too, but she didn't admit it."

"Did Tilly have a weekend job?"

"Yeah, she did a bit of babysitting for a couple of kids in Oak Street I think. It wasn't very often but they paid okay. She said the children were alright, not too much trouble so it was easy money and she got to read in peace when they went to bed."

Anna felt she'd got everything she could from Belinda and thanked her for her time. The girl had her face back in her book before Anna had even moved away from her. She'd wanted to stop and speak to Mrs Hathaway again, but her phone started ringing so she waved her hand and went straight outside to take the call.

It was her superintendent and he didn't even wait for her to speak before telling her what he wanted.

"DI Moore, a dog walker has just come across a blue sneaker just off the road that leads to Oak Street. It was hidden by the grass on the verge before you get into that field. A search team is already on their way and I need you to drop everything and join them immediately. The sneaker was stained with blood so it's not looking good."

The phone cut off before she could answer, but Anna remembered full well who had on a pair of blue sneakers when they missing. Her father, Jim, had been adamant that she'd always worn them.

Daisy owned a pair of baby blue sneakers that were her pride and joy.

15

Chapter Fifteen

Julie hadn't given him an unwatched moment since he'd decided he needed to check the shed. It was as though she knew what he was planning and had decided to keep an eye on him.

Chris opened the news app on his phone, he'd found himself compulsively scrolling through it in case there was anything about Daisy. So far he hadn't come up with anything, but it didn't stop him constantly looking and refreshing the page.

Today, however, there was a headline that caught his eye.

Missing Tilly Thorpe – Police now believe that the missing schoolgirl didn't make it out of Newton and have moved their search to here. Superintendent Young told us, "It's early days in our investigation but please be assured we'll be turning over every stone and following up on every lead until we find Tilly."

"Julie, have you seen the news on that missing kid case?"

She glanced up briefly before searching up the story on her own phone. After a quick read through she smiled at him.

"About time we got a bit of good news! At least if they're focusing on Tilly they won't be as interested in Daisy which is good for us. A missing child trumps an adult every time."

He looked at her in horror and she shook her head in puzzlement.

"What's eating you now? It's almost as though you're looking for the doom and gloom in everything. This is great news Chris, the best."

"How can you be so pleased a child is missing? Are you some sort of monster?"

Julie sighed and spoke to him with the exaggerated patience of an irritated parent to a child who just wasn't getting it.

"I'm not happy Tilly's missing, that's not what I'm saying. I'm happy that the police will have other things to focus on apart from Daisy."

To Chris, it felt like the same thing. She could dress it up any way she wanted but it sickened him that she saw this as a positive. Looking at her calm face and how she'd already turned back to her constant texting he felt a wave of anger so fierce it took him by surprise.

Right now he could cheerfully kill her with his bare hands. He'd always known she was calculating, but this was beyond the pale. His eye alighted on the sharp knife he'd been using earlier. It would be so easy to pick it up and use it. He could picture himself slitting her throat so fast she didn't have time to react. He thought about the blood splattering the screen of her phone and decorating the cream walls.

Clenching his hands into fists to stop himself carrying it out he stood up and snatched up his keys. If he didn't get out of the house right now he'd kill her.

"I'm going for a drive."

His announcement didn't elicit anything more than a casual nod in his direction so he took his anger and his dark thoughts and stormed out of the house.

In the car, his thoughts veered from fear of the police discovering what they'd done to wondering who Julie was having an affair with. The way she spent every waking moment on her phone it must be serious. Chris moved Marcus into the top spot of suspects. He didn't know why but there was something about the way they'd looked together that made him sure he was the one.

He'd take the old road through the fields, he decided. He'd not driven that way since the accident, but it was a useful shortcut and he liked the idea of not meeting any other traffic. Besides, maybe it was time to take a look around and make sure they hadn't left any evidence behind, he thought.

The road wasn't in the greatest state of repair. The council had limited funds for works and a small backroad wasn't on their list of priorities for the small budget they had to spend. His car bumped and bounced through a few potholes and he found himself swerving around as many as he could. The road was wonderfully empty until he got almost to the point where the accident had happened.

Coming over the hill he hadn't been able to see what was happening on the other side until he came over the brow. It was at this point that he almost drove right into the collection of police vehicles parked on either side of the road. Winding down his window slightly he could hear shouts, whistles, and the crackle of police radios as uniformed officers and sniffer dogs marched across the surrounding fields.

Was this to do with Tilly? Would they inadvertently find Daisy while they were looking for her?

And Julie keeps telling you there's nothing to worry about, she's playing you, Chris. Just you wait and see.

An officer approached his car and motioned for him to wind his window right down. Chris's hand shook as he pressed the button to lower it and the officer leaned right in.

"Good morning sir, can I ask where you're headed today?"

Chris swallowed, his mouth was suddenly dry and his heart was pounding so hard he was surprised the officer couldn't hear it.

"I live back there, on Oak Street. I sometimes use this road as a cut-through to town. Is there something going on officer?"

The officer scrutinised him for a moment before stepping back and muttering his registration into his radio. Returning to the car he eyed Chris with that suspicious look common to the police.

"I'll need your full name and address please sir, we're keeping a log of everyone who uses this road regularly."

"Christopher Knight, 23 Oak Street."

Chris produced his driver's licence and the officer gave it his full attention before stepping away to speak into his radio again. Closing his eyes for a moment he prepared himself for what was bound to happen next. He'd be arrested, handcuffed, read his rights, and then thrown into the back of a police car. At the station, he'd get checked in and be allowed his one phone call. Who would he call? Julie to warn her? Would he be better using it to get legal assistance or should he just use the duty solicitor like they did on the tele?

As the officer walked back to the car Chris tried to read his intentions in his blankly professional expression.

"Thank you, sir, that'll be all. If we need to ask you anything we'll be in touch."

Chris sat there unable to move until the officer impatiently waved him on, reving his engine more than he'd intended he roared away. Chris carried on driving until he was out of sight, then he pulled over and got out his phone. He'd been intending to call Julie but instead ended up doing another obsessional scroll through the local news site.

New evidence in the Daisy Landsbury case – A police source has told us that a piece of potentially vital evidence has been found in a local field. Superintendent Young won't confirm that a blue sneaker was found by a dog walker late last night. Daisy's father is quoted as saying, "My Daisy loved those shoes, it's definitely what she was wearing when she went out that night."

He was pretty sure he was about to vomit. His morning coffee was swirling around his stomach and burning a sour path back up the way it'd gone in. Jumping out of the car he bent over by a tree and took deep breaths until the moment passed. He had to get back to Julie and tell her because despite how pissed he was with her she was the only one he could talk to.

He was going to have to go into town and then home the long way around. If he went back past that police officer he'd start to wonder why Chris had cut his journey short. It felt like it took forever. Every light was on red and the other drivers were arseholes who plodded along, didn't know where they were going, or cut him up constantly.

Slamming into the house he almost ran into Julie who was pushing a vacuum around the carpet while she sang tunelessly at the top of her voice.

How the fuck can she be this calm and happy?

Chris yanked the plug out of the socket stopping the machine dead in its tracks. He saw Julie bite back her sharp response when she caught sight of the look on his face. Not trusting himself to speak he thrust the phone at her open to the news story and watched her expression change as she read it. This time she wasn't so blase he noticed. This time she didn't brush him off like an irritating fly.

"Fuck, fuck, fuck."

Chris took his phone back before she dropped it.

"Yes, Julie. Fuck is very accurate. What do we do now? Didn't you notice the bloody shoe come off?"

"Why would I notice?"

Chris threw her a scornful look, "Because you were in charge of holding her feet that's why."

Julie went pale, her legs wobbled and she staggered back to sit on the stairs. Putting her face in her hands she took several shaky breaths before looking back up at him.

"What were we thinking, did we actually think we'd get away with it?"

The panic in her face and voice did nothing to reassure him, if even Julie didn't know what to do they were screwed. She leaped to her feet and shoved her shoes on. With a wild glance in his direction, she ran out of the door not even bothering to close it behind her.

Chris tried to catch her, he reached for her arm but his fingers barely brushed her as she raced by and down the drive. He stepped out considering going after her but stopped when he saw Rose Brent watching. Chris waved to his nosy neighbour, putting on a fake smile and going in and closing the door.

Leaning against it from inside he tried to think rationally about what to do next. What was Julie playing at?

Maybe she's gone to the police? Right now she's probably running along that back road looking to flag down the first officer she sees.

Chris blinked and tried to clear his head and that was when he remembered what he'd wanted to do next time he was home alone. Pulling on his own shoes he marched up the garden to the shed where he got the key from its hiding place and let himself in.

He didn't have to look hard to see it. One black bag in the far corner of the shed was completely untouched. The other bag was gone.

Told you, Chris, she's been planning to set you up for ages.

Chris distinctly remembered throwing it in that corner, but just to make sure he opened the top and checked the contents. Yes, his clothes were in there and Julie's were nowhere to be seen. Picking up the bag he decided to burn them right now while he still had the opportunity.

Striding out he was about to dump the lot in the metal can when a familiar voice called over the fence.

"Please don't light a fire Chris, it's the first chance I've had to do some washing for ages."

Bloody Rose.

She always seemed to show up at the most inconvenient moments. The problem was if he argued the toss and insisted on doing it anyway she'd remember it. He could hear her now, telling the police about how he'd burned something just before they'd come to arrest him.

"No Mrs Brent, I'm not planning on burning anything. Is that all or can I get on with my day now?"

Rose glared at him, "Why are you always so rude young man? Rude, selfish, and arrogant, the same as everyone else your age."

Chris decided the best play was to ignore her. Maybe she'd get bored and sod off back indoors to stir her cauldron or poke pins in her husband, or whatever it was the old witch did for fun. For once it worked, Rose humphed and then disappeared from view.

Chris eyed the black bag, he couldn't burn it here so what should he do with it? He couldn't put it back in his shed, he needed to get rid of it.

What would the police say if they came across evidence you'd been burning things anyway? You need to get it as far away from here as possible.

That was true, maybe it was a good thing Rose had interrupted him after all. He'd put the bag in the boot of his car and then take it in the middle of nowhere to burn it. Before he could second guess his own decision Chris hurried out front and stuck the bag in the boot of his car. He'd just shut the it when Julie appeared.

She was out of breath as though she'd been running.
Or maybe she'd popped off to see her fella for a bit of nookie?

He ignored her and marched back into the house with Julie on his tail. As soon as they were indoors she blurted out what she'd been thinking about.

"I went for a walk and a think. Chris. We've got no choice but to hand ourselves in. I don't care what you do, but I'm going to the police and I'm going to tell them everything."

16

Chapter Sixteen

Anna smiled at Dr. Balfour, "You're potentially my favourite forensic lead right now."

Teddy eyed her with amusement, "Since I'm your only one that isn't the greatest compliment, but I'll take it with good grace."

She looked down at the wad of handwritten notes that Teddy and his team had painstakingly photocopied and encased in individual plastic envelopes. The writing was exacting, printed, and scrupulously neat, much as the person who'd written it had been.

Who'd have guessed that Agatha kept a log of everything she observed while spying on her neighbours from the window in her lounge?

"We noticed that some of the pages from her recent entries are missing and from the jagged edges of the paper, I'd suggest they were torn out in a hurry. Possibly by someone who broke into her home to get to them."

Anna nodded, that gave credence to her theory that someone else had been at Agatha's house the night she died, and it looked as though this was what they'd been after. What had Agatha seen that someone had gone to such lengths to hide?

Teddy cleared his throat, "And that's not all. We have a definite set of prints that aren't Agatha's. If you can find a suspect we can compare them and have the burglar bang to rights."

Anna chuckled, "Very good Teddy, you're clearly getting the hang of the terminology."

The doctor grinned back before giving her a sweeping bow and exiting the room. It looked as though her gut feeling had been right, someone had broken into Mrs Cross's home and even if they hadn't actually pushed her they'd caused her death.

Anna was eager to get reading the diary entries, laying them out on the table she made sure they were in date order. Before she could make a start on it DS Bridges tapped on her door looking very much like a man with a lot to say. As soon as she beckoned him in he bustled through the door and plonked himself on one of the chairs.

"You look full of it Neville, manage to wheedle anything out of creepy Mr. Angel?"

DS Bridges waggled his hand from side to side, "Kind of. I mean, he didn't exactly confess all but he did feel comfortable sharing some of his views."

Neville pulled a sour face. A short, stocky man with the beginnings of a beer gut, he always looked untidy as though he didn't look after himself. It was an act, however. Neville had perfected the art of looking so innocuous that witnesses and suspects would end up confiding all sorts that they wouldn't tell any other officer. One of his specialties was being able to get under the skin of sex offenders. She was sure it wasn't a skill that Neville would've wished for, but he made full use of it in the fight to bring them to justice.

"To start with he was definitely a bit cagey, and he's 100% got the hump with you. Once he got into the swing of it I had chapter and verse on what a bitch you are."

Anna grinned at him, "And I suppose you found it impossible to disagree with his analysis?"

"Only in the spirit of building trust with him of course Boss."

They shared a good-natured chuckle before he continued.

"I'll have to say right off that I would not be happy if he was teaching my teenage daughter. In fact, I'd probably rip his nuts off if he so much as looked at her. He's got this aura about him, you know the one, they all have it."

He was right, Anna thought. Once you'd met a few sex offenders you soon started picking up on those little red flags that you never used to notice. It even invaded your day-to-day life. She'd once stood behind a man in the supermarket queue and although they hadn't spoken she'd seen how he looked at the young girls and read his body language all too well.

Obviously, you couldn't pre-emptively arrest anyone, but Anna had got a photo of him and run it through the system. She'd found out he was a known sex offender with a liking for underage girls. Then she'd let the officer from the Jigsaw team that oversaw those on the sex offenders register know what she'd seen. That triggered a search of his accommodation and turned up enough evidence to recall him for the rest of his sentence.

It didn't always work out like that, but she tried to focus on the saves not the fails where she could.

"So, did you get anything concrete out of him?"

"It was mainly reading between the lines boss. His face got that sick expression when he talked about Tilly and Daisy and he was quick to agree with me when I introduced a few "ideas."

Anna knew what he meant. It was a trick he used to good effect. He'd buddy up to the suspect and start making the odd comment that suggested he thought in a similar way. Nothing overt, nothing that could make them cry entrapment, but just enough to get them comfortable with him.

"He described a very different Tilly to everyone else. According to him, she was a wild kid who partied hard and had an older boyfriend that she sneaked off to meet."

They exchanged a look and he nodded, "Yep classic case of him wanting to blow his own trumpet without actually telling me directly. I'd guess that the older boyfriend was him. Either in his fantasies or if we're really unlucky, in real life."

DS Bridges hefted himself up out of the seat and Anna hid a grin. He always moved like an arthritic geriatric, but he seemed to forget she'd seen him chase down a teenage boy without breaking a sweat. Neville had a carefully cultivated persona that he wore like an old overcoat. Unobservant people dismissed him with barely a glance, but those who bothered to look closer saw glimpses of the real DS Bridges underneath. They noticed the gleam of intelligence in his eye, and that under the slight beer belly, he was physically fit and capable.

Fluttering his fingers at her he called out goodbye and plodded out of the door. After he'd gone Anna leaned back in her chair and pulled Agatha's diaries towards her. Flicking through and scanning for familiar names she noted the occasions that she'd seen Tilly and Daisy on the street. It'd be worth checking if any of those coincided with them babysitting or in Daisy's case, cleaning at Tom's place.

Another note of interest was the wife of that strange guy from number 23, Christopher Knight. Agatha had made a few notes about her and apparently, she was sure the woman was having an affair.

Putting them aside while she checked the incident logs for the search team she spotted the list of vehicles that had been stopped going by. One in particular sprang out at her.

Christopher Knight.

He was definitely someone that she should speak to again, his name just kept cropping up. The next email made her put Mr. Knight to one side. The initial tests on that sneaker were back and the blood type matched Daisy. They still needed to do the full DNA testing, but she'd eat her hat if that shoe didn't belong to the missing girl.

The Thorpes had reluctantly agreed to see Anna at the same time. Dad, Keith, sat as far away from his ex-wife, Mandy, as possible. They'd managed a cold civility right up until Anna had asked about Mandy's new partner.

Keith glared at her, "who is this bloke Mandy? How do you know he's not some pervert that's done something to our little girl?"

Mandy threw him a scornful look, "Pete isn't a pervert and he hasn't laid a finger on Tilly. I don't see how you think you've got the moral high ground either, the only reason we're not together is because you couldn't keep in your pants."

"Oh, here we go, throw the past in my face why don't you? And it's not the only reason. I wouldn't have strayed at all if you weren't such a cold bitch."

Before Anna could intervene to pull the conversation back to the reason she was actually here Mandy spat out her retaliation.

"Pete doesn't think I'm cold, must've been that you didn't know how to treat me."

Anna raised her voice slightly to be heard over Keith's angry response.

"That's enough! I want all of this leaving outside the room. The only important person here is Tilly and us finding her, which I can't do without your help."

Both parents stopped, and Keith looked down at his shoes in shame.

"Sorry DI Moore, what must you think of us? For me, it's the guilt that makes me lash out. Mandy's right, I did cheat. I threw my marriage and my family away for a woman who dumped me just after I broke up with my wife."

Mandy looked surprised, "Why didn't you tell me? I thought you two were still together?"

"No love, she dropped me like a hot potato the second you chucked me out. I think she was just in it for the thrill of sneaking about and didn't fancy the reality of me full time and being stepmum to my kid."

The atmosphere in the room lightened and Anna felt they were finally in a place where they could get on with the important task of the day. Finding Tilly.

"So, what was Tilly's relationship with Pete like? Just to reassure you both I've run him through the system and he hasn't got any history we'd be concerned about."

Mandy looked uncomfortable, "If I'm honest Tilly wasn't keen at all. Not because Pete did anything wrong, but she was still hoping me and her dad would get back together. I think she saw Pete as getting in the way of that. She wasn't rude to him, she just went out whenever he came over. I could kick myself for not putting her first. I should've just finished it, she wasn't ready for me to be out there dating again."

Keith shook his head, "She'd have settled down Mand. You've got to get on with your life much as it pains me to say it. If anything, it's my fault. If I hadn't put off calling you for so long maybe we'd have found her by now."

Mandy shifted her chair so she was close enough to her ex-husband to pat his hand reassuringly.

"No point in what ifs and maybes now Keith. Maybe if I didn't jump down your throat every time you called you wouldn't have put it off."

Anna was touched by the way they'd pulled together after the acrimonious start to the interview. They hadn't really given her anything in the way of leads as she'd hoped, but at least they were able to support each other.

"Do either of you know if she had a boyfriend?"

The two parents looked equally bemused and shook their heads. Mandy sighed before giving a small smile.

"Not that we knew of. She spent all her time reading with her best friend Belinda. She didn't really seem to go to the sorts of places where she'd meet up with boys."

It'd been a long shot, as a rule, teenage girls didn't share that level of detail with their parents but it was always worth asking. The next question would need to be worded gently, she didn't want them jumping to conclusions.

"What about school? Did Tilly have any anxiety about going back, was she bullied, or did she have problems with any of the teachers?"

Keith looked at his ex-wife, "To be honest I wouldn't really know, Mandy dealt with most of that stuff. I went to a couple of parent meetings, her form tutor spoke highly of her so I think she was doing well."

Mandy nodded, "That'll be Mr. Angel. He was always very complimentary about Tilly and her achievements. She didn't have many friends. Mostly it was just her and Belinda, but she wasn't bullied either as far as I know. She liked being in Mr. Angel's form and was looking forward to going back. She thought he was "dead cool for a teacher." I was just pleased she had a nice form tutor."

Mrs Thorpe dabbed her eyes with a balled-up tissue and this time it was Keith who reached over and squeezed her hand.

"We'll get her back love. The police will find her and she'll be home before you know it. I can promise you this Mand, if I find someone was involved in this and they've hurt a hair on my girl's head, I'll swing for 'em."

Anna read the truth of his threat in his suddenly flinty eyes and the pulse that throbbed in his neck. Keith Thorpe suddenly didn't look like a devastated father, he looked like a man who'd kill someone with his bare hands if it got his daughter home. She couldn't blame him either. It was how most parents would react, and for her, it solidified her belief that he had nothing to do with Tilly's disappearance.

Chapter Seventeen

Chris stared at Julie as fear churned his stomach like a washing machine.

"What the fuck Jules? It's too late for all that, they'll want to know why we kept quiet so long."

Julie hunched her shoulders over and shuffled her feet, but when she looked back up her eyes were clear and he could tell her decision was made.

"They'll find her anyway Chris and it'll be worse for us if we wait for them to come and get us. At least if we hand ourselves in we'll get to tell our side of the story."

She means her side. She's going to spill her guts and make sure they put the blame squarely on you. She'll be fine, it'll be you that gets sent down, you that they'll all hate.

The voice was right, he'd be the monster who killed a young girl whilst too drunk to drive and then threw her body in a hedge for the wildlife to eat.

He noticed Julie was looking at her feet as though she had something more to say although he couldn't think what could be worse than what she'd already said.

"I need to tell you something else Chris. You're not going to like it, but there it is. After you told me about Agatha I snuck over there to find out what she knew. I had a look through her notebooks and you should've seen what she wrote about us. And not just us either, everyone in the street."

He looked at her in horror, "You didn't murder that old lady did you? Jesus Julie, what the absolute fuck?"

Julie tried to look contrite, but he could see the don't care attitude all over her face.

"I didn't kill her, what sort of a monster do you think I am? The stupid old bird fell down the stairs and broke her neck. I heard the crash and when I went to look there she was. All crumpled up, her head twisted too far the wrong way, and bits of broken china all around her."

Chris stared at her incredulously, "You didn't call an ambulance? You just left her there?"

Julie rolled her eyes at what she clearly perceived as his refusal to understand the situation.

"Oh yeah Chris, I thought I'd call 999 and explain that while I was breaking into her house she fell down and died. No officer it was nothing to do with me."

Her sarcastic tone made him clench his fists.

"Your a mercenary bitch aren't you? And while we're on that topic perhaps you can explain why I found the bin bag of my clothes unburned in the back of the shed?"

Her face dropped slightly and that nerve started twitching next to her eye.

"Don't start with the paranoid accusations again. I'd only just got mine done when that nosy cow next door started staring over the fence. I was going to sort yours out next time I had a chance to."

She's lying Chris, I know it and you know it. She's not even very good at it. At least you know now, at least you know what she was planning.

"Come on Chris, let's put all this childish arguing aside. We're going to need to stick together from now on. It'll all feel better once we get it off our chests. All this guilt, that's what's causing all these fights."

Chris pulled a sad face and nodded, "You're right, there's no point dragging it out Jules. We'll go down the station together."

His wife looked relieved and Chris wondered what was going on in that head of hers. Was she already ticking over with ideas of how to frame the whole thing so she came out of it relatively unscathed?

There's only one way out of this now Chris. You know what to do, but have you got the guts?

Julie was already bending over to change her shoes, clearly eager to get going to the station so she could dob him in.

She'll tell them you were drunk, she'll make out you threatened her and made her go along with it. She'll turn on the waterworks and they'll believe her.

He couldn't have that. It was bad enough that he'd killed a young girl but for the world to think he was an abusive husband who'd scared his wife into going along with it? He'd be hated, and when he went to prison he was fairly sure there'd be a line of people wanting to give him a battering.

Chris shuddered, could he really go through with it? Could he actually kill Julie? Despite everything she was still his wife and once he'd loved her very much.

Julie turned and gave him a smile, actually to Chris, it looked more like a smirk. In fact, he was pretty sure that he caught a certain smugness in her expression.

"So, maybe we should get our stories straight? How should we play it?"

Chris used a casual tone that he knew would lull her into a false sense of security. Julie was always happy to win, and she must feel as though she had him exactly where she wanted him right now.

"I think we need to stick as close to the truth as possible. It was dark and wet, visibility was poor and we didn't even see her. She probably ran right out in front of the car. We both panicked and did the stupid thing of hiding her body but now we want to come clean."

Chris nodded as though agreeing with her.

"Do you think I should mention that I'd been drinking?"

Julie hesitated, and it was that hesitation that sealed her fate. Chris could see it all over her face even as she shook her head.

"There's no point bringing that up. The restaurant will confirm that neither of us drank much and they won't know about the alcohol you had at the house before that. It's too late to do a drink-drive test." She's definitely planning to say something. She'll tell them all about it

and when they find your previous conviction that'll be that for you.

Go directly to jail, don't collect £200.

"I know we haven't been getting along lately Jules, but how about a hug? I'm shitting it here."

He could see her calculating how to play it and deciding that holding him was worth the prize of getting rid of him once and for all. She'll be glad to be shot of you. She'll be off with her fancy man before

they've finished turning the key on the cell door.

Julie held out her arms as she approached, but before her traitorous hands could touch him he grabbed her around the throat. Her eyes widened with shock as she realised what he was about to do. She struggled, but he kept his grip and pressed down with his thumbs as hard as he could.

Julie's eyes bulged, her breath was coming in short gasps now and he was surprised at how good it felt. All that dreaming about killing her off and now, he was finally doing it.

Her feet kicked out at him but she had very little strength to fight back and he easily moved out of her way as he continued to apply pressure to her neck. It took longer than he'd thought it would. She held onto life as long as she could, but finally, her eyes glazed over and she slumped against his hands.

When he let go she crumpled to the floor like a rag doll discarded by a thoughtless child. He looked down at her, wanting to feel something, anything, that would suggest he'd done wrong. Instead, all he felt was relief that it was all over.

Now he had to deal with her body. He could hardly leave her to decompose on the hall carpet. He considered his options, it was probably best to get her as far away as possible. He still had that bag of clothes to burn so maybe he could kill two birds with one stone. He could put her in the boot and find an isolated place miles away to get rid of it all. That way it'd be over once and for all.

Chris grabbed a black bin liner from under the sink, he'd line the boot with it and then dump her on the top. Going out to the drive he was relieved to see there was no one about for a change. Clicking his zapper he popped the boot and laid the bin liner inside before nipping back to the house and scooping up Julie. He managed to roll her in before slamming the boot door with a little more force than he needed to.

Right, the next move was to get out of here and find a nice spot to deal with the evidence and Julie, he thought.

"Mr Knight, can you spare a moment please?"

The voice belonged to DI Moore, Chris froze right next to the boot. Had she seen him putting something in the back? Would she ask to see it, and if he refused would that make her more suspicious?

"I haven't got long DI Moore, I was just going out."

Chris was pleased to hear that his voice didn't tremble in the slightest, he sounded a lot calmer than he actually was. He could feel the beads of sweat bubbling on his forehead and he knew if he looked down his hands would be shaking.

"I won't be long, just a couple of questions and if possible I'd like to speak to your wife too."

18

Chapter Eighteen

The way he'd slammed the boot down as she walked up the drive made Anna think Chris had something to hide. Everything about him was sketchy, from the sweat trickling down his face to his trembling hands.

"Are you okay sir? You don't look too well?"

Chris shook his head, "I've had a terrible stomach bug DI Moore, I'm only just getting over it."

"Sorry to hear that Mr. Knight. I'll try to be quick. Is your wife around?"

Asking about his wife seemed to make Chris even more sweaty, she thought with interest.

"She's still got the bug officer. She's in bed and I'd rather not disturb her."

Anna felt she didn't really have much choice but to let that one go, but made a note to herself to come back at some point and try and catch the elusive Julie Knight.

"I really just want to know what you were doing the night Daisy Landsbury went missing. I know she was seen in the area and you regularly use that road where her shoe was found so I wondered if you'd seen anything that might help us?"

Chris mopped the sweat off his brow with his sleeve.

"I remember that night, we went out for dinner. We'd have been home by about ten thirty latest."

Interesting, thought Anna. According to Rose, Agatha had seen them come back at gone midnight. There was something cagey about the man, something she didn't like.

"I also heard that you had a falling out with Agatha before she died?"

Chris shrugged at her, "Not really a falling out as such. I don't like to speak ill of the dead but she was a nosy gossip who was trying to find out why the police were in the street. I thought she was being insensitive to the young girl who's missing and gave her short shrift. Agatha wasn't pleased and marched off to complain about me to my neighbour Rose."

That all sounded very planned out, she thought, but unfortunately, it was also plausible.

"Did you know that Agatha kept notes on everything she saw in the street?"

Chris looked as though he was going to chuck up. His face paled and he dropped his eyes.

"Is that all DI Moore?"

Unable to think of anything else Anna shook her head, as she left she noticed that far from rushing off in his car, Chris went back into the house.

Anna decided to cover all bases. Sitting in her car in a layby near the search of the fields she used her time to read through Agatha's notes. The woman was spiteful, vindictive and judgemental. Every word oozed with poison. From her observations that Julie Knight wasn't going to book club as her husband thought to her certainty that it meant she was having an affair.

All through the notebook she speculated on who with and had a neat list of suspects that included Tom Angel.

And there he is again, thought Anna.

Agatha had logged Daisy and Tilly being on the street and which houses they went to. Again, she followed on with a few comments on the laziness of young families nowadays and how they'd entrust their children to "just anyone."

She had the same unpleasant views on most of the street. The neighbourhood children who she terrorised and yelled at, and their parents who she thought were "namby pambies." If it did look as though Agatha's death had been murder the suspect list was going to be as long as her arm.

The missing pages covered the period when Daisy and Tilly had disappeared, which Anna felt was too much of a coincidence. She was musing over who would be the most likely person to want those notes when she heard the searching officers shouting.

The sky had darkened and Anna suspected another storm was brewing. The heat had become oppressive again and she hoped a downpour would cool things down a bit. Striding across the field towards the row of officers she could see they'd stopped still and were moving into a semi-circle around whatever they'd found. Anna pushed her way through them and followed their eyes down towards an overgrown hedge.

A small, grey hand poked out between the branches, and the cuffs of a dirty, dark blue hoody had ridden up. The small, daisy tattoo on the inside of the wrist confirmed this was the missing girl.

The rest of her was hidden from view behind the jumble of branches and leaves, and Anna wondered what they'd find when they pulled her out. Daisy had been decomposing for nearly a week in the heat, and that was without the likelihood that the local wildlife hadn't been dining on her.

There was silence among all the officers. No one ever got used to finding bodies, especially when it was a young person or child.

Teddy Balfour led his team over and gently asked the officers to step back so they could erect the white tent and start their work. Everyone moved reluctantly as though they wanted to stay and protect her for as long as they could. Anna understood how they felt, but their job now was to get Daisy justice.

Chapter Nineteen

He couldn't believe his bad luck.

First that DI Moore shows up and almost catches him putting Julie in the boot, and if that wasn't bad enough when he finally got in the car he found it was low on petrol. Chris slammed his hands on the steering wheel in frustration, the last thing he needed was to stop at a garage to fill up. He had no choice though, if he didn't it'd be even worse to run out in the middle of nowhere.

He could just imagine being stranded in the countryside, miles from home, with a body in the boot of his car. Better that he take the less risky option of stopping off and filling up.

That detective was clearly suspicious if her questions were anything to go by. As for Agatha Cross, if she wasn't already dead he'd have pushed her down the stairs himself. What the hell was she thinking of, logging everyone's comings and goings? How bloody dare she?

He was starting to understand why Julie wasn't in the slightest bit put out by Agatha's death. Nasty, vindictive old cow.

The local garage was quiet, with no queue of people waiting to fill up which was a welcome relief. Maybe his luck was on the upturn finally?

Chris pulled his card out ready to pay at the pump so he could fill and go, then he stopped. Using his card would leave a paper trail that'd come back to bite him if anyone ever checked. Better to pay cash at the till, keep his head down and hopefully no one would recognise him.

Decision made he pulled out the nozzle and filled up to the amount of cash he had in his wallet. In this day and age of contactless card payments, he rarely needed "real" money and rarely bothered to draw any out of the cash point machine. When he was done he ducked his chin into his chest so the shadows covered as much of his face as possible. He needn't of bothered, the lad behind the glass in the kiosk barely bothered looking at him as he rang up the total. Chris put the money in the slot underneath and waited impatiently for his receipt to be printed.

It was the cashier who alerted him to the next piece of bad luck, in fact, bad luck was a weak description, it was catastrophic.

"Hey, mister, that bloke's nicking your car."

Chris turned around just in time to see the rear of his car as it zipped out of the station and onto the main road. In his hurry to fill up and get on his way, he'd left the keys in it and some little reprobate had taken the opportunity to pinch it.

What the fuck was he going to do? Some joyriding little shit was currently speeding around the county with his wife's body and a bag of evidence in the boot. If he got pulled over or decided to have a poke about in the boot it was all over.

"I've called the police, they should be on their way. Don't worry we've got CCTV I bet they'll find out who took it in no time."

Great, really great. He hadn't thought of CCTV, not that it mattered, far from slipping in to grab some petrol he was now the focus of everyone's attention. He'd have to style it out. If he cleared off now the police would be even more suspicious about why he didn't want to work with them to get his car back.

Thieving little fuckers, if he could get his hands on the little bastard he'd be putting him alongside the treacherous Julie. Taking a seat on the bench outside the kiosk he tried to distract himself by scrolling through his phone. Far from keeping his mind off the current situation, it served only to ramp up his anxiety when he found the local lead story.

Body found in hunt for missing Daisy Landsbury – Police have refused to speculate on the identity of the body found in Palmer's fields earlier tonight but sources close to the case have told The Tribune that it's a young girl who matches Daisy's description.

Bloody marvelous, that was it then. No matter how careful they thought they'd been Chris was pretty sure there'd be some trace of them on her body. It wasn't as though they were master criminals, just an ordinary couple who'd had the misfortune to accidentally run someone over.

When the uniformed officer approached, Chris was half-tempted to confess all. There was no way he wasn't going to be found out at this point and maybe Julie was right about getting the opportunity to tell his side first.

And what good will that do you? You've come this far, hold your nerve
  for a bit longer.

PC Coles was efficient, but it was clear to Chris this was a crime that he dealt with day in and day out. He noted the car's details and the times of the offence in his notebook and offered no reassurances that they'd get the car back.

"The most likely outcome sir is that when they're done they'll burn out. I'm sorry not to give you a more positive outlook but I don't want to offer false hope. They all do the same thing, sir, run the car ragged and then take it to an isolated spot to burn it out so we can't get any evidence of who took it. We generally know the likely candidates, but knowing and proving it are two different things."

Chris was initially outraged, when even the police had no confidence in their own ability to catch criminals the world was clearly going to hell in a handbasket.

> But won't it serve your purpose if someone else burns the car out along with the body and the evidence? No link to you and they take all the risks. So long as they don't look in the boot it should all work out just fine.

That was true, he thought with renewed hope while giving the officer a disappointed sigh.

"Is there really no chance that you'll pick them up before they burn it out and get my car back to me?"

PC Coles shrugged, "I'm not saying it's impossible, but it is unlikely. I like to be upfront and that way if you do get it back it's a nice surprise but it avoids you pinning your hopes on it happening."

Chris narrowly avoided laughing out loud. If anything he was hoping the officer was right and that the joyriding little bastards inadvertently did his dirty work for him.

Misreading Chris's expression for mocking annoyance PC Coles added, "TWOC is a crime on the increase sir. As soon as new safety measures come out the kids find a way around it. They don't even sell them or strip for parts, they just rag it around the estate flashing it off for their mates before burning it out."

Chris could hear the frustration in the officer's voice, "I understand officer, I really do. I'm more annoyed with myself for not being more careful."

That seemed to do the trick, the officer gave him a nod and thanked him for understanding the situation. The whole thing was starting to feel surreal, just over a week ago he'd thought the potential end of his marriage was the biggest problem in his life. Since then he'd killed two people and was pretty sure he was about to spend the rest of his life behind bars.

If by some miracle he did get away with it how was he going to live with what he'd done? He'd spend the rest of his life looking over his shoulder, waiting for the day when the police finally snapped the handcuffs on and read him his rights.

Maybe he should hand himself in? It wasn't too late, the officer hadn't left yet, he was still at the kiosk picking up the CCTV.

You killed Julie to stop her from going to the police but now you're planning to do just that?

The voice made sense and Chris decided he was better off seeing how it played out. Pulling out his phone he called a local cab company and booked a ride home.

Chris finally struck lucky when his cab driver turned out to be one of the rare few who didn't want to make conversation and allowed him to silently fret about what might happen next. He was so grateful that he added a generous tip when he tapped his card details into the portable machine.

He couldn't help taking a quick look around as the cab pulled away which was why he noticed Rose at the end of her drive staring at him. The lid of her wheely bin was open suggesting she'd been putting out the rubbish when she'd spotted him arriving.

Chris was sorely tempted to flip her the bird and tell her to fuck off, but not wanting to add to what she potentially saw as suspicious behaviour smiled and waggled his fingers at her instead. Rose snorted loudly before slamming down the bin lid and stomping back into her house.

Miserable cow, every time he wanted a bit of privacy there she was. Staring and judging.

"Evening Chris! Everything okay?"

It was Marcus, great, thought Chris in irritation. Just what he needed right now. Not.

"Hi Marcus, all good, just a bit of car trouble."

Marcus nodded, but seemed distracted, "Haven't seen Julie about today? Not like her."

Chris felt that worm of suspicion creeping through his thoughts, since when did Marcus keep track of Julie's movements?

"She wasn't too well earlier but luckily she recovered enough to go to book club. I'm sure she'll be home soon."

Marcus frowned, "That's odd, I usually see her heading out to her club. Maybe I missed her.."

He drifted off as though he wasn't sure what else to add.

"Must've done, what a shame, I'll let her know you're asking after her."

There must've been a sharpness to his tone that he didn't intend because Marcus threw him an anxious look.

"I don't mean anything by it, Chris. Just making conversation here."

Chris tried to smile but was pretty sure it didn't look in the slightest bit friendly. He actually felt sick at the thought that his so-called mate was now the most likely candidate for his wife's lover.

Indoors he kicked off his shoes and poured himself a large scotch. He was suddenly exhausted, completely wiped out by it all. This had quite possibly been the longest week of his whole life and now he had no one to talk to about it. Julie may have been a nasty bitch who was potentially banging his best friend, but she'd also been the only other person he could share this shit with.

20

Chapter Twenty

Lewis had found the rest of his crew in their usual spot outside the chicken shop on the high street. He'd pulled up and sounded the horn which was their cue to jump in. Marvin and Jonny in the back and Felicia in the front. As his girlfriend she got pride of place in the front seat next to him where he could bask in the admiring looks of pride she shot at him.

The car was a decent ride and Lewis pushed his foot right down to demonstrate to his passengers what it could do. The powerful car shot through a red light causing Felicia to squeal in excited fear, a sound that urged Lewis on to ever more risky manouvers.

Once on the estate they knew like the back of their hand he raced the car down side turnings and handbrake turned around the car parks. Some of the curtains around them twitched with nosy residents taking a peek to find out what the noise was. Lewis was confident that no one would be foolhardy enough to call the police though. People around here knew what happened to grasses and he'd be surprised if anyone took the risk.

They'd had the car a couple of hours when Felicia started complaining she was bored.

"We've done the whole estate and the owner's bound to have called the old bill by now. Let's dump it."

Lewis knew she was right, but he was enjoying his moment in the spotlight. Usually, it was Melvin who lifted the decent cars but just for once lady luck had shone her bright light on him. He'd just been strolling past the garage when he'd seen the car and couldn't resist the urge to have a look in the window. He'd been hoping to spot something worth nicking on the passenger seat and was shocked, and delighted, to see the keys dangling from the ignition.

No one left their keys in a car anymore, this was literally unheard of making it a gift it'd be rude to walk away from. Lewis had jogged quickly around the driver's side, let himself in, and before the car owner had a chance to notice had roared off down the street.

The others had joined in now, "Yeah come on Lew let's go burn the fucker out."

Lewis sighed. This sort of chance wouldn't come up again any time soon, but he had to face facts, it was time to do the deed. Stopping briefly at Melvin's house to collect the bottle of fuel he had stored in the garage they gave the car one last spin out to the fields. Felicia was unusually quiet as they pulled up.

"This is right next to where they found that girl's body isn't it? Don't you think we should go somewhere else?"

Lewis laughed at her, "Don't be soft."

Embarrassed by her boyfriend's mocking laughter Felicia didn't say anything more but she hung back from the others as they poured the fuel over the outside of it and a healthy glug on the seats inside.

"Let's have a look in the boot and see if there's anything worth nicking."

This was from Jonny who always had his eye on the prize. Lewis popped the lock and they all huddled around as the lid lifted.

It was Felicia who saw it first, letting out a scream that turned Lewis's blood cold.

"What the fuck? Do you want half the fucking police force to come running you stupid bitch?"

Felicia didn't answer, she just pointed a shaking finger at the boot where the body of a woman was curled around a large black bin liner.

The three boys just stared at it in silence, while Lewis wondered at how his luck could turn sour so fast. The first time he got the opportunity to shine and it turned out the fucking car owner was some sort of serial killing psychopath.

"Shit. What're we going to do about that?"

Melvin stepped up, physically the biggest of the group and the most criminally experienced it was always him they turned to.

"We burn the fucker out as we planned. It's not like we can call the police and report it, the fucking car has our dabs all over it so they'll know it was us in a second. Then what do you think they'll do? They'll pin all of this on us, that's what."

They all nodded in agreement, even Felicia.

Melvin took charge. Flicking the flint on his clipper he lit the edge of a petrol-soaked rag and then threw it through the open window so it landed on the back seat. They all stepped back, time and experience had shown them you didn't get too close because when it blew you could easily end up catching light yourself.

The flames curled around the seats first and as they ate away at the petrol spread quickly until the whole of the inside was ablaze. Watching the fire was usually something that Lewis enjoyed, it gave him a buzz, but this time he couldn't shake the thought of the woman in the boot. They were basically cremating her as well. He looked at Felicia, tears streaked her face and ash landed in her hair.

He put an arm around her, "Come on Flick, don't be like that."

As they turned away and started the long walk back to the estate Lewis heard the boom of the car exploding behind them.

Chapter Twenty-One

DI Moore pulled up outside 23 Oak Street.

Her team of uniforms and of course her DS were all waiting for her to give them the word. They weren't expecting too much of a battle to take Chris Knight into custody, but you had to be prepared for anything.

When the local community officer had found the burnt-out car on the field he hadn't thought much of it at first. The field was a popular place for the local scallywags to dispose of the cars they'd nicked and various patches of scorched grass marked each previous spot.

Sighing to himself at the amount of paperwork this was going to create for him he popped the boot. Sometimes he'd find items unburned inside that'd give him a clue as to the owner so he could let them know. Looking inside he wasn't sure what it was at first. Peering down for a closer look the smell of charred flesh made him retch. Stepping back and taking some gulps of the clean air to hold back the vomit he pulled out his radio and contacted the station for back-up.

DI Moore had gotten wind of it when the serious crime email had pinged up on her phone. Immersed in what had now become a murder investigation she'd been tempted to ignore it, but her quick scan paid off when the car owner's name jumped out at her.

Chris Knight's stolen, burned-out car had been found in the field next to the one where Daisy's body had been hidden. That in itself wouldn't have set her juices flowing, but the body found in the boot had.

They'd have to wait for an identification, but the pathologist had gone out on a limb and said he was 90% certain it was female. Anna had tried to push him on an age range but Dr Balfour wouldn't be budged on that.

"No way DI Moore. If I so much as hazard a guess it'll be in far too wide range to be of any use to you. I know you suspect this could be Tilly Thorpe, and I imagine you're hoping it isn't, but I can't confirm either way on the spot like this."

Anna was irritated, not with Teddy per se but at how right he was about her feelings on it. However, a body was still evidence of a suspicious death whoever it belonged to, and the car owner needed questioning.

Chris had answered the door to her with an irritated expression that turned horrified when he saw the army of officers behind her. Anna had given him her sweetest smile, the one she'd been told was annoyingly smug, and pulled the cuffs off her belt.

She'd insisted this collar was hers, she'd put in the graft and she should be the one to take him in. Chris stiffly did as he was told as she clipped the cuffs on and read him his rights. When she got to the point of "on suspicion of murder," she thought he was going to pass out.

His mind must've been whirring with questions because he didn't say a word all the way to the station and once there he spoke only to confirm his name and answer the questions the duty sarg asked him. He looked stunned as he was led to the cell and handed a blanket.

"Anything else we can get you, sir?"

The uniform waited and eventually, Chris gave a small nod, "Any chance of something to read?"

"I'll see what I can do."

Anna watched as the door was slammed shut and locked. Chalked on the board outside were the words.

C Knight – Murder

She wasn't sure how to feel about it. Part of her was pleased at catching him, but what murder had he committed? Who was the body in the boot of his car? Although Anna was desperate to find Tilly she was hoping it wasn't her.

⋙ ⋅⋅◆⋅⋅ ⋘

Chris had requested a duty solicitor so they'd had to wait to speak to him until they'd shown up the following morning. He'd been allocated Joe Collitt who did not look best pleased when he walked into the station. Anna had heard that he tried to avoid cases involving children and he must be wondering if this had anything to do with Tilly.

Joe seemed more confident when he led his client into the interview room and Anna did the introductions for the benefit of the tape. Waiting until she'd finished he announced that his client had made a statement and wouldn't be saying anything else.

"I'll read it out and that's all you're getting until we see a bit more evidence as to why my client's been arrested."

Looking smug he cleared his throat and made a production of starting.

"My car was stolen from the garage whilst I was paying for my petrol. During the time it was missing the thieves had full access to the vehicle including the boot. I have no history of violent offences and as such ask why you are not considering that these known offenders are not responsible for the body you state you found in my car."

Joe eyed Anna as though waiting for her response, but she knew better than to feed into his dig for information. This was all about him pushing to find out what they knew and hadn't yet disclosed to him.

"Thank you Mr Collitt. I will now go through my questions. Your client may not wish to answer but it's my duty to ask them and give him the opportunity to tell me his side if he wishes to."

Joe nodded and shot a look at his client reminding him to keep to the no comment rule.

"Mr Knight, or would you prefer I call you Chris?"

Chris looked at his solicitor but without waiting for his advice shrugged, "Chris is fine."

Anna could see Joe was annoyed at how easily Chris had spoken up. The point of no comment was to use it throughout the interview including the seemingly innocuous questions the police asked.

"So, Chris. As you're aware a body was found in the boot of your car. It's currently with forensics and they're working hard to identify it and see if there's an obvious cause of death. Do you know who's body that is in the boot of your car?"

She could see Chris was a talker and he was already having difficulty not firing back answers.

"No comment."

"Is it your wife, Julie?"

"No comment."

"Is it Tilly Thorpe?"

This time there was a pause as a look of disgust passed across Chris's face.

"No comment."

"Where were you going last night, Chris?"

Chris tapped his foot against the floor and glared at her.

"No comment."

"Was your wife having an affair Chris? Is that why you killed her?"

He screwed his eyes closed as though willing her to have disappeared when he re-opened them.

"No comment."

"So, you aren't denying murdering your wife then?"

Anna liked to chuck a firework into the room every now and again, especially when a suspect used the no-comment response. Joe answered her before Chris could break his silence.

"That's unfair DI Moore and you know it. No inference of guilt can be made from someone using their right to silence."

Anna grinned at him enjoying the look of annoyance he shot her in return.

Joe sighed heavily as though bored by the whole process, he flicked his wrist so his cuff moved up enough for him to glance at his watch.

"So, how long are you intending to hold my client? You haven't disclosed enough evidence to charge him so I'm not sure what the point is of holding him any longer."

There was a huge clock mounted on the wall that Joe could've looked at, his use of his watch was purely theatrical and Anna had seen him play the same game before.

"We're well within our allowed time for holding Mr. Knight as you're well aware. So, let's all take a break and we'll reconvene in two hours once Chris has had some breakfast."

As soon as they'd left, Chris escorted by two burly uniforms, Anna's face lost its confident smile. Joe was right, she didn't have enough for the CPS to charge him. Until they had a name for the victim he could argue he didn't know who it was and he hadn't put it there.

"DI Moore? There's a man asking for you at the front desk. A Marcus Pollock."

That name rang a bell, she thought, but she wasn't sure where from. Since she was still waiting for forensics to come back she may as well find out what he wanted. Knowing her luck he'd turn out to be one of those nutters who were always making false confessions.

The man himself didn't look like a false confessor, he looked like a guy who'd diverted from a run to pop into the station. He was wearing baggy shorts coupled with a form-fitting sports top and top-of-the-range trainers and was slightly out of breath as he waited for her.

Holding out her hand she introduced herself, Marcus gripped it gratefully and explained who he was.

"I'm a neighbour of the Knights, umm, I heard you'd arrested Chris and wanted to share a concern with you."

He looked around the busy reception. As usual, it was bustling with a mixture of people waiting their turn. Realising that he might want a little more privacy, and hoping that whatever he'd come in to say would give her some leverage, she guided him through the security door.

Once they were sat in an empty interview room he burst into his reason for coming in as though he needed to get it off his chest before he changed his mind.

"This isn't easy DI Moore. Firstly I need to tell you that I was having an affair with Chris's wife Julie. We'd been seeing each other for a few months and we'd got to a point where we were talking about leaving our respective partners and making a go of things properly. Anyway, last night she was supposed to meet me to give me the green light. We'd agreed we'd then go home and do it at the same time. The thing is she didn't show up."

Anna could see the worry etched across his face.

"I know this is difficult sir, but is it possible she just changed her mind?"

Marcus nodded despondently, "I thought the same thing so I took the risk of sounding Chris out. The thing is, he told me she'd gone to book club as usual which can't have been true. Book club is just something she made up to get away to see me."

This was getting more interesting, she thought, if Julie was missing it was entirely possible it was her body in the back of the car.

"What makes you suspect Chris? Do you think he knew about the affair?"

He blushed, "Julie said he was paranoid and making a load of accusations and kept trying to follow her whenever she went out. She tried to lead him off the trail by heading for different houses in the street and she was fairly sure he hadn't sussed us."

Anna nodded, "So you think he suspected the affair even if he didn't know who it was with? Does he seem like a man who'd do something violent to his wife if he found out?"

Marcus shook his head, "I've never known Chris to be aggressive in the slightest, but he's not been himself lately. He seems all on edge."

Her phone buzzed quietly in her pocket and she quickly checked the screen. Seeing it was Dr Balfour she tapped out a message that she'd be available in five minutes.

"Sorry Mr. Pollock, I've really got to take this call. Thank you for coming in and I'll be looking into your concerns."

Marcus looked relieved to be getting away and with a hasty goodbye and thank you couldn't wait to get out of the room.

"Hi Teddy, it's Anna. What have you got for me?"

"The body is Julie Knight. We confirmed with hairs from her brush found in the master bedroom during the search after her husband's arrest. In addition to that we investigated what remained of the other items in the boot. From the melted plastic it appears there was a black bin liner and it contained clothes. The fabric scraps are of good quality so I can confidently hazard a guess that these were going out clothes."

He paused, and she could tell he had something more for her.

"We also ran a routine check on her prints. It wasn't easy getting them but fortunately for us, the way she was positioned meant she was laying on one hand. That protected it from the fire enough that it was relatively unscathed."

Anna tutted impatiently, "And? Did you get a match?"

"We did indeed. Julie's prints match the unidentified ones we found in Agatha's house. I'd say you've found your intruder."

Anna thanked him, well this was a turning point. He was going to find it harder to stick with his unknown body that could've been put there by anyone story now. The other question was the clothes, were they the ones he was wearing when he killed her? If so why was he dressed up as though going out?

She'd also have to deal with the additional information that Julie had been the one to break into Agatha's house. Was it just to keep her affair quiet or had there been more to it?

"DI Moore, sorry to bother you again, but you've got another visitor at the front desk. Young girl this time says her name's, Suzy Croft."

Anna nodded, "Could you put her in one of the interview rooms please?"

There was another turn-up for the books, everyone seemed to be lining up to come clean.

Anna sent the email and the evidence to the CPS requesting permission to formally charge Chris with the murder of his wife. When she'd done she wandered a couple of doors up and found Suzy sitting with an older man in an interview room.

Suzy looked up, her cheeks were streaked with dry tears and she rubbed her nose on her sleeve before speaking.

"DI Moore, I've got something really important to tell you."

22

Chapter Twenty-Two

The older man in the room turned out to be Suzy's father. He gave his daughter a gentle smile and patted her hand.

"I know it's probably not usual, Suzy being an adult and all, but I promised her I'd support her through this and I'd like to keep my word."

Anna nodded her consent, this sounded too important to take the risk that she'd clam up if her father had to leave the room. She knew she'd made the right decision when Suzy took a deep breath and clutched her dad's hand.

Suzy was scrolling through cat videos and people doing stupid dance moves when Daisy called. She leaned back as she answered it, sprawling out comfortably ready for a long gossip, but instead, all she could hear was the sound of Daisy sobbing.

Sitting up, panicking, she asked what was wrong. Daisy was barely coherent through her sobs.

"Oh Suze it's bad, it's really, really bad. I need you, I don't know what to do."

Suzy's heart sped up, Daisy was the sensible one of the group it had to be something really bad if she was this upset.

"What's happened?"

All she could hear for a moment were heart-wrenching sobs.

"I can't tell you over the phone, I need to see you. Meet you by Palmer's field."

The phone had gone dead. Suzy yanked on her clothes and shoes and let herself out into the storm. She'd pulled on a waterproof but it wasn't doing much to keep her dry as the wind whipped the rain into her face. Putting her head down against the painful sting of water on her skin she reminded herself that Daisy would do the same for her.

By the time she'd reached the road that wound past Palmer's field her feet were squelching inside her trainers and her hands were numb. Up ahead Daisy was just an outline under the tree backlit by the moon. She looked agitated, pacing up and down and glancing around her as though scared she was being followed.

As soon as she saw her friend Daisy threw her arms around her, and Suzy rubbed circles on her back like her mum did for her when she was upset.

"Oh Suzy, I've been so stupid."

They'd moved further under the tree where its sturdy branches offered some shelter from the driving rain.

"Do you remember Mr Angel from school? You know I clean at his house, well, we started seeing each other, but earlier he sent me a really weird message ending it. I was at the pub picking up my wages, I wanted to get him a birthday present you see. Anyway, I went straight to his house to have it out with him, I thought he was seeing someone else. It was so humiliating, he wouldn't even answer the door even though I knew he was in there."

Suzy stared at Daisy in horror as her friend gave a huge sniff and wiped her eyes with her sleeve.

"I got really mad, the least he could do is tell me to my face right? So, I crept around the back of his house to see if I could see him through the window and make him talk to me. The curtains were all drawn up tight and I couldn't see in. I was going to tap on the glass but then I heard this weird noise. Like a thumping and crashing sound from the end of the garden. It was coming from the shed so I went for a look."

Daisy's voice sounded almost hysterical at this point and she was having trouble getting her words out.

"There was this kid in his shed. She was all tied up and gagged. I wanted to call the police but when I got my phone out I heard the back door and knew he was coming so I ran for it. I saw Mr. Wilk at the end of his drive and flagged him down. I thought he'd help me. I was about to try and tell him what I'd seen when he grabbed me and tried to kiss me. It's sick Suze, all of it. Mr Angel, Mr Wilk, who do we trust anymore? They only care about one thing and we need to make sure they pay for it. We've got to go to the police station Suze and tell them before he hurts her."

Daisy was looking expectantly at her friend but wasn't expecting the reply she got.

"You're lying! Tom wouldn't bother with someone like you and you've made up this stupid story just to split us up and get him in trouble."

Daisy took a step back, "How long have you been seeing him?"

"Ages, since I was at school off and on. It's me he loves and just cos you fancy him you think you'll be in with a chance if you break us up."

Daisy shook her head, "Suzy, no. I'd never make up something like this. Come on we've got to go to the police."

Suzy grabbed her friend's arm, "Stop it Daisy, stop telling lies right now."

Daisy stepped backwards trying to pull away from her friend's grip.

Suzy was crying and her dad handed her a tissue, she took a deep breath and wiped her eyes.

"She caught her heel on a tree root, I let go and she fell right into the road. There was a car coming and it hit her head on and bounced her over the bonnet. She was lying all crumpled on the ground and I think I knew she was dead but it was like I was frozen and couldn't move. The car stopped and a man and a woman got out, I thought they'd call for help and I wouldn't have to let on I'd been there. They had an argument and the man told the woman he'd been drinking. Then they picked her up between them and took her off into Palmer's field. I got scared, really scared. I thought if they knew I'd seen them they'd have to keep me quiet so I ran home."

Suzy glanced at her dad at this point as though seeking his reassurance and he stroked her hair.

"It's okay Suze. Tell DI Moore all of it, you've got the worst of it out of the way."

The young girl nodded and continued the story.

"The next day it was like I dreamed it, that was until I heard Daisy was missing and her parents were frantic. The problem was the longer I left it to say anything the harder it got to admit to it. Then you interviewed us all and I thought that was it, you knew what I'd done. I was even too scared to ask Tom if it was true so I've just been staying away from him."

Suzy looked down at the tabletop, "I lost my best friend and I didn't even get to keep the man that I thought was worth it."

Her dad looked at Anna, worry lines scored his face, and gave him a haunted look.

"It was an accident officer, just a tragic accident. If anyone's to blame it's the people that ran her over and just threw her in a field. Not forgetting that pervert teacher, he's got a lot to answer for."

Anna was already on her feet, "Before we can go any further with Suzy Mr Croft I need to send officers to Mr Angel's home. For the time being Suzy needs to stay here where she's safe and I'll be back as soon as possible to talk more about where this is going."

Suzy's father nodded his agreement but Anna barely saw him as she rushed out of the room.

Chapter Twenty-Three

They didn't bother with the niceties of knocking, they just put his door through with the big red key. At the same time, another group of officers had busted the lock on the gate leading to the back garden to get to the shed.

Anna had gone with the back garden team. She wanted to be among the first to get to Tilly. All the noise around her faded as she waited to find out if the kid was dead or alive. The shed door gave way easily under the weight of the officers and Anna took a deep breath as she followed them inside.

The small figure at the back of the shed wasn't moving. Despite all the noise they'd made getting in there was no response.

Tilly was propped up against the wall, her chin touching her chest and her head slumped forward so her long blonde hair covered her face. Anna couldn't see her chest moving. They were too late, she berated herself. She couldn't believe she'd walked by this shed a hundred times and not known anyone was in there.

"I've got a pulse marm."

Anna sent up a quick thank you to whoever was listening. One of the uniforms was already requesting an ambulance attend urgently so she hurried over to the girl.

"You're safe now Tilly. We've got you."

Tom Angel had been taken by surprise when the officers had burst into his home. In a panic, he'd thrown the laptop he was using out of the window as officers tackled him to the ground and snapped the cuffs on his wrists.

He'd screamed, shouted, and protested his innocence even as he was led out to the police van. Tilly was raced to hospital as police and forensic officers took over the house for a thorough search.

Anna had been torn between staying at the scene and seeing what was turned up and going to the hospital with Tilly.

Tilly won.

She stayed in close contact with her Sargeant who she'd left monitoring things at Tom Angel's house. It meant she already knew what he'd been looking at on his laptop, no wonder he'd tried to get rid of it, she thought. it was full of pornographic images and videos of young teenage girls.

Tilly had come round fairly quickly once the doctors had given her some fluids. She'd been dehydrated and hadn't eaten properly since she was locked in the shed. Anna had offered to give her time to recover before questioning her but Tilly had bravely insisted on doing it right away.

She was sat up in bed, one parent on each side of her clutching a hand each as though if they let go she'd disappear again.

"It all started at school, Tom would keep me behind after form and talk to me like I was an adult not a child. He said he enjoyed our conversations and I was more mature than the other girls my age. I was really flattered by his attention, I don't have many friends and it was nice to feel special. Then he suggested that we start meeting up outside of school where we could get to know each other away from everyone else. He said it was better no one knew about our friendship because they wouldn't understand. "They'll make it seem dirty Tills." That's how he put it and I was so stupid I believed him. I started lying to everyone, saying I was visiting dad when I wasn't just so I could sneak over and see him."

Tilly's eyes filled with tears and her dad squeezed her hand, "We've talked about this Tills. None of that matters now you're back here safe with us."

He looked away and Anna saw the rage he was hiding from his daughter.

"I'd like a minute alone with that fucking pervert."

His anger seemed to comfort Tilly, maybe it gave her a feeling of safety, but she seemed to feel more able to continue.

"The day it happened I'd decided to surprise him. It was nearly his birthday and I thought I'd just turn up with a present for him. I didn't want anyone to see me so I went around the back of his house. I looked in the window, he had his back to me and was scrolling through these horrible pictures on his laptop. Hundreds of girls my age and younger, all of them naked and looking scared. When he heard me scream he turned round and then ran outside. He grabbed me before I could run, tied me up, and locked me in the shed. I don't think he knew what to do with me after that. If he'd let me go I'd have told but he couldn't bring himself to kill me either. Then I saw that other girl looking in and he went after her too. Did he kill her?"

Tilly's eyes were as wide as saucers and she looked relieved when Anna shook her head.

"He didn't kill her, but she is dead. I don't want you to hear it from anyone else, but she had an accident while she was getting away from him."

Tilly looked confused and Anna saw her mum stroke her head gently and murmur comforting words in her ear. She'd be okay, this was going to stay with her and there was going to be a need to talk to her about the nature of her relationship with Tom Angel. She hadn't said it out loud yet, but Anna was fairly sure it would turn out to be a sexual relationship in which case she'd be wanting to add charges to the mounting number that Angel was already facing.

Forensics had gone through Daisy's phone which had been found in her pocket. They'd already highlighted the call she'd made to Suzy, but also the numerous text messages between her and Tom Angel going back seven years to when she was only fifteen years old. He'd have a job denying it all, but he was currently using his right to silence and giving a "no comment" interview.

Anna was sure that once this went viral other girls would come forward and that they'd only scratched the surface of Tom's offending.

She also needed to deal with Christopher Knight.

It was like Tom Angel had thrown a rock into a pond that night. The ripples had led to Suzy pushing Daisy, Chris, and Julie hitting her, and ultimately Julie's murder. There was one ripple she hadn't gotten to the bottom of yet, Agatha Cross. Fingerprint evidence pointed to Julie having gone in, possibly to find the notes about her affair, but with both women dead Anna would never hear the whole story. She surmised that Agatha had heard Julie downstairs, picked up a vase for self-protection, and then fallen down the steps. There was no evidence anyone had pushed her or murdered her, but it was sickening that Julie had just left her there at the bottom of the stairs and run off. Not that there was anything she could do about it now.

However, this played out, whether Angel confessed or not, he was being charged and would most likely spend a long time behind bars. It should've felt like a positive outcome, but Anna couldn't help feeling saddened by the whole case.

There was also the personal angle. Tom Angel had taught at her niece's school and her next task was to let her know that she couldn't hold her secret any longer. Tasha would need to make a statement about his behaviour and it was better that her mum heard it from Tasha first.

Plus, Anna had another visit to make before Tasha. She needed to speak to the one other person who had played a part in Daisy's death and was probably thinking he'd got away with it.

It was a lovely, clear, sunny day and Paul Wilk was in his front garden kicking a ball back and forth with his son when she showed up. He hadn't noticed her at first, not until she'd cleared her throat behind him.

Anna saw the colour drain out of his face and how his hand trembled as he picked up the ball and handed it to the young boy.

"Bobby, can you take this to your mum please? I need to speak to this lady for a minute."

Bobby grinned at her, he was a small, stocky little boy with chubby legs and a cheeky smile. Paul Wilk watched him as he ran into the house clutching his football, waiting until he was out of earshot before turning to Anna.

"How did you find out?"

She shrugged, "Daisy told her friend what happened, and then she eventually told me. You've got a daughter haven't you?"

Paul blanched and looked as though he was going to throw up.

"That's not fair DI Moore."

"It's absolutely fair Mr Wilk. How would you like it if your Carrie needed help and when she approached an adult she should've been able to trust he breached that trust in the way you did? Daisy was someone's daughter Mr Wilk. A father is out there devastated at her loss, and you played your part in that. If you hadn't of tried it on with her she'd have told you about Tilly. Not only would Daisy still be alive, but Tilly would've been home ages ago."

He shook his head as though trying to deny his culpability, and she wasn't surprised to hear another batch of excuses.

"I don't know what came over me officer, I'd never have dreamed of doing something like that before and I can promise you I never have either. It was just seeing her there in the rain, it was as though she wasn't real and it was just a fantasy. I was putting the rubbish in the bins when she showed up, she waved to me and then came over. She wasn't really dressed for the weather and her clothes were soaked through and clinging to her. I'd had a few beers with dinner and, well, I just reached out for her. It's not as though I broke any laws though is it?"

Anna shot him her best glare, it was a cold look designed to tell the recipient that she wasn't buying what they were trying to sell. Paul got the message as he trailed off.

"Your actions that night led to one girl dying and another nearly doing so, if you think you're just walking away from it then you're sorely mistaken."

Anna got her cuffs out as she heard Mrs Wilk approach, she waited until his wife was in earshot before reading his rights.

"Paul Wilk, I am arresting you on suspicion of manslaughter. You have the right to remain silent, but it may harm your defence if you do not mention anything that you later rely on in court. Anything that you do say may be given in evidence. Do you understand the caution Mr Wilk?"

The harsh sound of the cuffs snapping onto his wrists was his breaking point. He tried to back away but she had a firm grip on his arm.

"No, no, no. You can't do this."

Anna gave him her coldest smile, "But I can Mr Wilk, and I have. It's anyone's guess if the CPS will go ahead with this charge, but in the meanwhile everyone will find out what you did. Even if you don't go to prison I will make sure you pay one way or another."

"Leigh! I need you to organise a solicitor for me, one of the ones you work for, whoever's the best."

His wife shook her head, "Paul, if you think I'm putting my reputation on the line because of your stupidity you need your head testing. Get a duty, and forget coming back here if you get bail. I'll leave your things on the doorstep, you can pick them up or the binmen will take them next visit."

Turning on her heel she stalked back into the house and slammed the front door behind her. Anna tugged on Paul's arm as she directed him towards her car.

"Either you come in with me without a fuss, or I'll call a van and you'll be taken kicking and screaming in front of all your neighbours."

Pointing up the street and giving a cheery wave at a watching Rose Brent she saw the last of his resistance cave. It wasn't guaranteed that the CPS would go with a manslaughter charge, she was pushing her luck there, but she was pretty sure she'd get him on reckless endangerment at the very least.

Holding the top of his head she expertly loaded him into the back of her car. Looking in the rearview mirror she could his wife was already piling up bin liners outside the front door on the porch. Other doors opened and people came out to watch and Anna wondered if there were any other dark secrets bubbling away under the surface of this ordinary street.

Chapter Twenty-Four

Chris sat in his cell and stared at the book he had open on his lap. He'd had plenty of time to think and his solicitor had given him some stark advice.

"I don't need to know if you're guilty or innocent right now Chris, but the evidence is mounting up and I'd suggest you consider putting forward any mitigating circumstances at the earliest opportunity. DI Moore is going to offer you one last interview before you're transported to remand. I strongly suggest you take it."

His first thought had been to carry on denying it, but common sense had won out eventually. He was tired, exhausted by the lying and by his restless night in the cell on the hard bunk. He just needed it to be over.

When the DI had marched into his cell he could immediately tell that she knew everything. It was in the weary disgust in her eyes and the sharply professional tone she spoke to him with.

Chris sat on the bunk wrapped in the rough, grey blanket as she told him the CPS had agreed they had enough evidence to charge him. He tried to listen as she listed his offences, but it all seemed to get muddled in his head after the word murder.

"Your brief is on his way and we'll be conducting one last interview with you before you're transported to HMP Newham. You will remain remanded in custody until your trial. I suggest you take this opportunity to tell us exactly what happened."

The DI didn't wait to hear an answer, she spun on her heel and left. As the door banged closed behind her a tear ran down Chris's face.

How had this happened? He'd gone from an ordinary man to someone looking at spending the rest of his life in prison. One stupid bad choice had led to all of this.

The faces of Daisy and Julie swam through his head. Dead staring eyes condemned him and soundless screaming mouths hung open as though about to speak their last words. If he had the courage he'd end it all now, take his own life, and face whatever was in store as his eternal punishment. He didn't even though a lifetime of tiny cells shared with the sorts of people he'd never rubbed shoulders with before awaited him.

Chapter Twenty-Five

Anna had accepted the commendation from her superintendent with a heavy heart. No matter how often she was told she deserved it and how well she'd done, it paled in comparison to the lives that had been ruined and the people who were left damaged.

Chris Knight was still on remand awaiting his trial. She'd heard he was on suicide watch in a single cell. The remorse and guilt had come too late and she had no sympathy to waste on him. The only credit she gave him was that he'd made a full confession and was planning a guilty plea. At least that spared everyone the trauma of giving evidence. She only hoped that the court wouldn't be lenient and that he'd spend the rest of his life behind bars.

Tilly Thorpe was being supported by both of her parents who'd put aside their differences to offer her a united front. She'd met up with the girl a few times and had been surprised to find how much she enjoyed her company. She was seeing a therapist and was trying to put the past behind her.

"It's not easy. I keep thinking about how stupid I was. If I hadn't got myself involved with Tom that other girl would still be alive. All of this is my fault."

Anna had reassured her as best she could, it was typical that the least culpable were the most likely to blame themselves.

"It's not your fault at all, if anyone's to blame it's Tom Angel. He was the one who put all this in motion."

Tilly had nodded, but Anna sensed she wouldn't be letting go of her guilt that easily. Hopefully, the therapist and her parents would eventually be able to help her feel less responsible.

Suzy's case had gone to the CPS who ultimately made the charging decisions. Anna had been pleased when they'd decided that it wasn't in the public interest to charge Suzy with any offences. One of the positives to come out of it was introducing Suzy and Tilly to Stephanie Harrington and her niece Tasha. They'd made their own support group of four, but she could see the numbers swelling as more and more girls came forward to speak out about Tom.

Tom Angel himself was also on remand. He was being held on the vulnerable person's unit following a spate of attacks and threats from the other prisoners. Tom still hadn't made a full disclosure, and even though the evidence they had was enough to send him down Anna would've liked to hear it from him. Without a confession and with him planning a not guilty plea it'd mean the victims having to take the stand and reliving their trauma. They'd be questioned by his barrister and their whole lives and vulnerabilities put on public display. The girls themselves had remained steadfastly determined to see it through and get the justice they deserved but Anna could see the toll it was taking on all of them.

The schools where Tom had taught were carrying out internal safeguarding investigations to find out how he'd managed to get away with it undetected for so long. Anna had been asked to oversee the local ones and was already planning recommendations that included supporting pupils to report concerns. It had really bothered her that the young people involved hadn't felt listened to or believed. Perhaps the schools found it easier to dismiss allegations than to accept that a member of staff was behaving inappropriately. Whatever it was, Anna was hoping to oversee some changes in practice.

That just left Paul Wilk. The sniveling excuse for a human being had cried all the way to the police station, all through booking and then all through her interview with him. The CPS were reluctant to press ahead with manslaughter feeling that the evidence was too flimsy, but her job was done in regards to ruining him. His wife had gone through with her threat to kick him out, and he was in hiding following threats of physical harm from angry members of the public. Maybe she'd get a charge on him, maybe she wouldn't, but he'd be punished either way.

Anna had also made it part of her routine to pop into the Winton Arms regularly. It was an okay pub, but her real reason for going was to make sure that Kelvin knew he was being watched. The message she'd whispered in his ear that day must've got through because she never caught him chatting to young girls again.

Her dress uniform was feeling stiff and uncomfortable. It wasn't helped by the unseasonably warm early October weather they were having and she was looking forward to getting home and changing into something more casual.

Anna had the rest of the day off. Her team had wanted to spend the afternoon in the pub toasting her success but she'd gently excused herself. It didn't feel right somehow, not with so much misery left behind.

She'd already decided where she was going that afternoon, there was someone who she wanted to talk to. Someone who needed to know there was closure for them.

The grave was easy to identify. The earth was still freshly turned and raw, and the gravestone was new and polished compared to the older ones on either side. Someone had recently been and left a bunch of fresh flowers and Anna added her own to the vase.

"We got them Daisy, everyone who did you wrong has been caught and punished. It won't bring you back, and my heart aches for your poor family, but I can at least give you all closure."

Anna leaned back on her heels. This was who she did it for, the victims who couldn't speak for themselves. To Anna, the best part of being a police officer was the ability to right wrongs and deliver justice.

Afterword

I very much hope that you've enjoyed reading this book as much as I enjoyed writing it!

If so, can I please ask you to consider leaving a review to share your feedback with other readers. As an indie author, it can be very difficult to get your work seen so anything you can do to help share my books with those who you think may also enjoy them would be greatly appreciated.

If you'd like to share your thoughts with me or ask any questions you can find me on most of the social media platforms and I'm always happy to hear from you!

@MgarciaAuthor

Also By

Dark Obsessions

<u>Psychological Thriller Series</u>
- The Love of His Life
- Still The Love of His Life
- Always The Love of His Life
- Roses for Christmas (Coming soon)

Horror

<u>Short Stories and Novellas</u>
- Tales of Darkness Drive
- Comeuppance
- Greed Box

Supernatural Thriller

Willow Weeps

Fiction

Becoming Bill

One man's journey into homelessness and his battle to overcome his past.

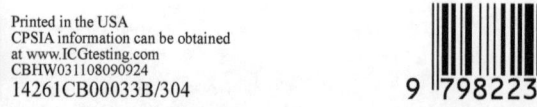